# THE OATH

## MADDY AND SILENUS

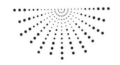

## SUSAN BADARACCO

*Dedicated to the Children's Advocacy Center of Denton County*

# CHAPTER ONE

 *ulsa, April 2011*

MADDY O'BRIEN WISHED her younger brothers would just get lost.

It wasn't fair that she had to walk them home from school each day so she purposely trailed behind...far behind. She watched as their twin heads leaned toward each others and assumed they were discussing *important* things, like the color of apples or the shape of a lower case 'g'. Their superhero backpacks bobbed up and down when they leapt over unseen objects and bent forward to examine a dead cricket. She fumed... a third grader shouldn't have to hang around kindergarteners.

When a truck swerved to a stop ahead of her, it caught her attention. She wondered if the driver might have some emergency. It wasn't until she saw the man approach her brothers on the sidewalk that the fear set in. He spoke to them. Gestured to the open truck door... and they *moved* toward it. He noticed her approach, urged the boys to move faster by pressing his hand against their backs. Maddy's backpack slid from her shoulders and crashed to the ground. She panicked.

"NO! Don't get in that truck!"

Maddy had never run so fast but she was still scared that she wouldn't make it on time. Her throat burned from her frenzied breaths and her heartbeat thudded in her ears, in pace with her pounding footsteps.

Tyler's whole body stiffened at her scream, he pivoted his head to find her and instinctively grabbed for his brother's hand. The two clung together, wild-eyed with fear, while the man propelled them roughly from behind. Each stumbling step brought them closer and closer to the open truck door.

Tyler grabbed his brother's ankle when the man lifted Tanner to place him inside of the cab. He tugged backward with all of his strength but lost his grip when Tanner began bucking and kicking in a struggle to break free. Tyler opened his mouth, let out a terrified wail, flung wild punches at the man's legs, but it made no difference. Undaunted, the man leaned forward toward the truck seat.

Maddy reacted without thinking and hurled herself at the stranger. She wrapped both of her arms around his bicep and drew it to her chest. His grip loosened on her brother when she forced him to take on her entire body weight.

Tyler gave up his futile assault on the man's legs, reached up and clasped his brother's wrist with both of his hands. In a desperate tug of war, he strained to pull Tanner free. Maddy pinched the underside of the stranger's arm, kicked his legs, scraped her nails across his face. He snarled back at her, but it worked… and his hold on the young boy slackened further. With Tyler's help, Tanner was able to twist free and jerk out of his captor's grasp. The boys almost toppled over, then froze, uncertain and confused, until they heard their sister's command.

"RUN!"

Maddy had a moment of relief to see them scurrying down the sidewalk, their hands tightly intwined. And then his head swiveled to face hers. Cold, bloodshot eyes in a bony face. He let out a hiss of frustration and Maddy released her grip on him, stumbled backward, but it was too late. He hooked his long-fingered hands around her upper arms and drew her closer. Maddy closed her eyes in dread, felt his putrid breath wash over her face. Her stomach turned over and bile rose in her throat. Her head felt like it was going to explode. Adrenaline flooded her body but despite her desperate struggle, her smaller size was no match for his greater strength.

The spray of frigid water startled both of them. Maddy opened her eyes to see a puzzled expression on the face of the stranger. Without loosening his grip, he looked up and over her head to identify the source.

"What's going on here?" a woman's strident voice demanded over Maddy's shoulder. More water burst from the hose, this time a direct hit to the man's face. His cheeks reddened, he let out a bellow of defeated rage, and Maddy found herself airborne when he savagely flung her out of his path. Maddy hit the concrete sidewalk, hard. For a moment, she felt nothing as her mind scrambled to make sense of what had just happened. But then she rolled over and all five senses came to life with exquisite intensity. Confused, she took a few breaths and felt her throat tighten as pain radiated from everywhere at once.

She fixed her eyes on the puffy white clouds that floated overhead and tried to ignore the metallic taste of blood in her mouth, the hot liquid that ran down her chin. Truck tires screeched on the road beside her. Pleading voices came from all directions around her, their sounds muffled as if she were underwater. Maddy watched with confusion as her frantic brothers clutched at each of her wrists and strained to pull her upright.

An older woman's face appeared in hers, followed by icy water spilling over her sprawled legs. Maddy blinked, tried to clear her head and the woman, finally, gratefully... flung the hose away. When her brothers managed to pull her half-way upright, her vision darkened, her knees buckled and she cascaded into her rescuer's arms.

Later, when the woman finished explaining to the police what she had witnessed, Maddy overheard her mom's hoarse whisper to her dad. "Oh my God, Dave, we almost lost them."

# CHAPTER TWO

 *ulsa, August 2015*

"MORE TEA, ROSE?" Emily O'Brien asked her aunt as she rose up from the dining room table balancing stacks of dirty plates. Hoarse shouts punctuated the blaring of the televised football game, overwhelmed the crackling of the fire in the hearth.

"Don't mind if I do," she answered, "why don't you join me a minute and then we can work on those dishes." Rose angled her body slightly and slipped off her shoes. She pulled up her feet onto the dining room chair next to her and let out a tiny groan as she felt her back muscles tighten and loosen again. Finally comfortable, she picked up her teacup and inhaled the soft steam. She took a tiny sip and practically purred in contentment. The dining room table was still covered with platters and silverware but Rose and Emily had a rare moment of solitude.

"What's the latest on the bookstore?"

Rose's eyes lit up and she leaned forward, "I think I have George talked into it. He was hesitant at first but he needs something to keep him busy now that he's retired. I've found the perfect place, right on Cherry Street, about four or five blocks from here."

"I'm so happy for you, Rose. I know that's always been your dream."

Rose nodded but then drew her eyebrows together. "What's new with Maddy? Have you thought any more about signing the two of you up for the self-defense class at the Y?"

"I keep changing my mind. I just don't know if it will help. She's such a worrier and I don't know how to fix it. She keeps tabs on the twins better than I do, Rose. For heaven's sake, they're practically as big as her, but she's still uneasy if she doesn't know where they are." Emily shook her head, took a sip.

"Do the twins ever bring it up?"

"Not often. But their conversations have always been, well... violent."

"Violent?" Rose's eyebrows went up.

"If I ever seen him again, I'm gonna tear off his arms and watch his blood squirt everywhere. Or...I'm going to kick him in the ...you know, boy talk."

Rose smiled wryly. "And Maddy?"

"She doesn't talk about it. She just stays home...all the time. I know she's lonely but she thinks all the girls her age are immature." Emily paused, struggled to find the right words. "I think she looks at the world in a different way now, like there's danger around each corner and every stranger is suspicious."

Rose paused, met her niece's eyes. "And you? Do you still have nightmares?"

The corner of Emily's mouth went up in a half-hearted smile. "Only rarely now, I'm doing much better. In the beginning, I worried she was picking up on my anxiety but I don't think that's true anymore. I'm really okay. I still might be a little antsy when the kids spread their wings a little. But Dave and I agree, we have to live a normal life, we don't want to raise paranoid and insecure kids."

Rose nodded in agreement, shifted in her chair. "How's the tennis league?"

Maddy turned away from the door frame and tiptoed up the stairs. She pulled her braid forward, removed the elastic tie, finger combed the thick auburn strands. Years had passed and she was still a *paranoid and insecure kid*. She flushed at the thought.

It was true. But it didn't have to be. She could change. She would sign up for the self-defense class with her mom. Maybe that would help. She had one niggling thought as she entered her room, closed the door behind her.

*Why can't I let it go like everyone else?*

# CHAPTER THREE

*R**ocky Mountains, April 1972*

"Nooooo!" The spike of the girl's adrenaline and cortisol were the tether that drew Silenus through time to where he stood now. The *incarnatus* was the call to action, an electric-like charge to his body that both enhanced his already monumental power and shot fiery pain to his core. He ignored the latter and concentrated on the scene that unraveled before him.

The girl was running for her life. She stumbled to a stop before him, then darted sideways, sobbing and wide-eyed. He winced. Once bonded, the incarnatus dictated that the human's emotional response produced a physical reaction in the unicorn. Fear and anxiety *hurt* the unicorns, a lot. But it wasn't his own pain he flinched from, it was the expression on her face when she looked up and saw a massive beast seemingly blocking her escape. Though the passage of time, the champion of the innocent had become a monster to be feared and now children ran *from* him instead of *toward* him.

Silenus took a moment, swiveled his head to search the area around him and try to determine who or what she was running from. Rocks skittered down the hill as she scrambled up an incline. He would lose sight of her if he did not move soon. He launched into a gallop. His massive hindquarters contracted and released, and he shot high into the air above her.

What he saw ahead made his heart falter. And then everything went dark.

His hooves landed on soft dirt instead of the rocky terrain he was expecting. Silenus stood still. Confused. His eyes focused on the familiar green of the training field and the soft misty spots that danced above it. His breath caught in his throat. An almost imperceptible quiver of his flank escalated until the tremor ripped through his body.

*He had failed.*

*Another of his charges was dead.*

Silenus' tail flicked violently once. Twice.

Vapor burst from his flared nostrils and his eyes rolled to the back of his head. His ebony mane belted the side of his neck as he thrashed. He reared up, and with muscular forelegs, sliced at the emptiness before him. Silenus stretched his neck upward and let out a furious roar of defeat that rent through the damp air.

# CHAPTER FOUR

ulsa, *September 2015*

MORGHAN SHELDON WAS A BUSY WOMAN. Her heels clicked on the wood floors as she led the movers carrying her husband's oversized desk into the study. She gestured the exact position with one hand, watching as they carefully angled the desk through the french doors, and finished up the conversation on her phone to connect the utilities.

Paperwork to enroll her daughter in school lay on the countertop ready to return. Public school, she thought with a frown, but she simply did not have time to investigate school options with her formidable schedule. She was meeting with a contractor to begin work on the exterior landscaping but she also had to call the internet company, again. Her checklist for the other house was even longer.

The cell phone in her hand chimed and reminded Morghan of her next task. Waving to the movers, she climbed in her car and made the short drive to the restaurant in Utica Square. Once parked, Morghan took a deep breath and pulled down the visor to examine herself critically. She slipped her hand in her purse, retrieved her red lipstick, dabbed it on her lips, all while remembering the first time she bought the expensive brand. It had been a turning point. Satisfied with her appearance, she clicked the visor shut and opened the car door.

Ivy laden columns marked the entrance and when she pulled open the heavy door, aromas of roasted meats and herbs greeted her. By the time her eyes adjusted to the dimness, the hostess stood ready to guide her to the reserved spot. Morghan inspected the table as she circled it. Satisfied with the arrangements, she smiled and greeted the ladies as they arrived behind her.

Moments after one of the women complained about her son's missing backpack, the table fell to a sudden silence. She looked around, puzzled, "It's not that big of a deal, we'll find it, it is the third time though."

"It's not what you said, it's what Morghan said…"

"What? What did she say?"

"Morghan, tell us again…"

Morghan looked around the table at the group of women she hoped to get to know better. "Blane and I opened a home for teenagers that have no other place to go."

"Are you kidding? Do you even have the boxes unpacked at your house? I thought you just moved in… I can't find my son's backpack in a normal household and you've started a shelter for teens?" Water spilled over the sides of the glass as she gestured emphatically.

"I wish I was that committed," another woman chimed in. "I've been so stressed out about the backyard renovation and meanwhile Morghan is working to save the youth of the world. I want to do something worthwhile…" she added with a wistful look.

"Why are you doing this?" the third woman asked.

Morghan drew her brows together and appeared to gather her thoughts. Her calculated pause drew their attention like moths to a flame. They put down their knives in the middle of cutting, their glasses in the middle of sips and leaned forward.

"Not long ago, my daughter and I were coming out of a department store in New York after a busy afternoon of shopping. Allison bumped into a panhandler and as I pulled her away, we both realized it was a girl not much older than Allison. She was confused by the whole thing, of course. Soon afterward, a classmate of Allison's was left alone after her mother ran off. Allison asked her father and I what was going to happen to her friend. Blane and I had no idea. The whole affair had quite an impact on all of our lives and we decided to do something. It can be quite overwhelming though."

It didn't take long for the women to react.

"I'm serious Morghan, give me your cell number and let's get together, I want to help you on this."

"I'm in too."

"Oh, okay, I'm in, but I really hope this means I will get more help with the annual sports fundraiser."

When the last of the ladies departed, Morghan sat alone at the luncheon table with the constant hum of quiet conversations continuing in the background. Waiters bustled around her, clearing salad plates, silverware and lipstick smudged glasses. She leaned back in the velvet upholstered chair, rested her head against the seat back and looked up at the crystal chandelier glittering over the table. A small smile teased at the corner of her mouth. *They loved her.*

~

BLANE SHELDON TOYED with the idea of entering politics. Success tonight might be just the thing he needed to put his foot in the door. On Morghan's advice, his grey dress pants and a white dress shirt replaced the suit he planned on wearing. He rolled up the sleeves and examined himself in the mirror. His hair, artfully highlighted, looked windblown and natural while his apparel spoke of a confident but hard working man. He arrived early and waited in the antechamber. A formality, he was told. Ten minutes after the start of the meeting, Dave O'Brien opened the door and invited Blane in.

Blane looked around the room, made eye contact with each person around the conference table. His easy smile generally won people over and tonight was no exception. Dave walked him to the head of the room and took the podium. "Blane, I want to personally welcome you to tonight's Alliance meeting. As we discussed previously, we are a group of men and women whose common goal is our service to the community. I would appreciate it if you would take a few minutes to describe to our members what your vision is and what you have accomplished so far."

Blane drew the bottled water to his mouth and took a quick sip as he strolled to take Dave's place at the podium. "I am honored to address this board and explain my goals," he began. "But, let me start by saying as driven as I am, I am relying on you to point out when I am going down the wrong path. Your passion and drive have made you each successful in the community and my contribution can only take on significance if I can learn from you and build on what started as a simple wish...."

Blane paused to look around the room again. A few faces stood out from his internet searches of the committee members. On his left was Thomas Markham, the volunteer president of the local institution that provided financial assistance to families in need and who created this "alliance" of the various charities of the community. The doctor representing the local health department was on his right, sitting by a representative of of the community justice program. Dave O'Brien smiled up at him as Blane glanced to the side. Dave was the president of the local food bank, a position he held for the last decade. He'd been Blane's first contact when he moved into the area. Blane knew representatives from the public library, the recreation center and the senior center were gathered here too.

"Childhood is a wondrous time right? I know that our daughter has been a true blessing in our life. I keep reminding myself that as we make this journey through her teenage years! Seriously, though, we've had it quite easy in our household compared to some. Orthodontist appointments, forbidden phone calls after bedtime, an impossible amount of potions for bad hair days, I thought I'd seen it all."

"But one day, my daughter came home from school and I heard her sobbing in her bedroom. Her science partner, her friend… had been abandoned by her own mother. The stress of a job loss and possible eviction was just too much for the single mother and she simply disappeared, leaving this child quite alone. My daughter asked me what was going to happen to her. I am embarrassed to say that I had no idea. No idea what happens to teenagers that suddenly find themselves without family support."

Blane let the thought settle. The hole in the network of organizations around him was the teenagers.

"Homeless youth are at a higher risk for abuse and drug problems. Some die in the streets. Most of these teenagers are too young to work, to drive… they really are in a hopeless situation. With my beautiful daughter in mind, I started to brainstorm what I could do. What these kids needed was simply another home, I thought. A door that won't be locked against them. A parental figure that would hold them accountable for their actions. Food on the table and clean sheets on the bed." Blane stopped and grinned, "Yeah, I was that naive!"

"Our first house has four bedrooms in Yorktown. It was a foreclosure that needed a lot of work but that allowed us to customize it for our needs. Three bedrooms each hold two girls and the last bedroom is for the house mother. Remodeling an older home can be crazy but that was the easy part." Blane grinned and shook his head. A few committee members met his eyes, nodded in agreement, and his smile widened even further. *This is easier than I thought.*

"I really do have a lot to learn. Things got complicated after opening the door for the girls. Keeping the boys and drugs out, keeping the kitchen stocked...all challenges that we have successfully faced. We filled up our spots pretty fast. We now have openings only when we lose one."

Blane slowed and looked down frowning. "I never dreamed that we would be less then 100% successful. But, I've learned that you can't save everyone and occasionally we have a teenager that leaves us. We keep an open door for these prodigal daughters but the goal is not to lose them in the first place." Blane could see the sympathy in their eyes as made the admission.

"I would not call our undertaking a success yet... but perhaps instead, an adventurous work in progress. We have taken a few girls off the street and now we are looking at another property so we can continue offering a safe haven to others. We are planning another girl's house since our research shows that most homeless teens are girls."

"By the way, I keep saying 'we'. My wife, Morghan, shares my passion for this project and in all honesty, she is the driving force, willing to do anything it takes to make this work." He looked around the room, one last time, and smiled sheepishly as he finished. "I know that what I have done is small compared to what all of you have already accomplished for the community, but I hope that you can see the promise of it, like I can."

Blane saluted with the empty water bottle, shook a multitude of hands as he wove through the room, and finally returned to the antechamber to allow the attendees to cast the membership vote. *They loved him.*

# CHAPTER FIVE

ctober 2015

TAFFY COLORED pinks and oranges glowed on the edge of the horizon as her parents loaded the SUV with boys and sports equipment. Maddy stood on the dimly lit front porch and observed the activity with a bagel in one hand and Zeus' collar in the other. "I think I'll stay here this morning. I might go for a bike ride." Her hand tightened imperceptibly on the collar as she waited for a response.

Her mom paused, shifted the case of water bottles in her arms before looking up at her in surprise. "Are you sure you want to stay alone, Maddy? Why don't you come with us."

Maddy's dad threw a tattered quilt in the back and patted his wife on the arm. "Maddy's getting older, it's fine if she wants to be alone this morning." He threw the last of the gear in back, reminded Maddy to wear a helmet and climbed in the front seat. Her mom hesitated, knit her brows together, stared at Maddy with a puzzled, concerned expression.

"She'll be fine, Emmie," he coaxed.

Her mom looked troubled but climbed in the front seat and shut the door. Her dad flashed Maddy a proud smile, pulled out of the driveway and turned down the street. Maddy was alone.

Maddy looked down at her bike and helmet dubiously. The helmet had rainbows and sparkly stars on it, and mercifully, no longer fit. The pink princess bike was made for a fanciful six year old and not a gangly twelve year old. Frustrated, Maddy turned and spied her mom's bike and helmet tucked behind the lawn mower and the extra set of golf clubs. The thick layer of dust meant her mom wouldn't mind if Maddy borrowed it. Maddy navigated it toward the driveway, wiped off some of the grime with a rag she found on the toolbox and slipped on the helmet. She pushed down hesitantly on the pedal, propelled the bike into the street. The helmet strap felt a bit snug under her chin and the gears made a funny noise as she shifted but with practice, the transitions went smoother.

*I can do this*, she thought. *I can let it go....*

Her body fell into a familiar pattern and a smile stole over her face when the wind buffeted her cheeks and pushed through her sweater. She pressed on the pedals harder now, enjoying the rush of chilled air, while still concentrating on weaving around potholes created by the past harsh winters. Leaves drifted down from overhanging trees and swirled around her tires in eddies. Tidy houses and tree lined parks whizzed by until finally, Maddy stopped and stretched out fingers that were stiffened in position around the handle bars. She flexed her hands, shoved the icy fingers up her sleeves and glanced around the unfamiliar neighborhood.

*I'm really doing this*, she thought, leaning back in her seat, grinning with pride.

A high-pitched yapping drew her attention and she

giggled at the ridiculous noise and tried to locate the dog in the otherwise quiet street. Her gaze went from house to house, searching for the barking animal, but it wasn't a dog that caught her eye.

Maddy was transfixed. It couldn't be *real*, not again?

Halfway down the block, two men were struggling with a teenage girl. One wore a black leather jacket and the other, an untucked thermal shirt with black boots. The girl was bare-footed, wore a gray sweatshirt and striped pajama pants. Her blonde hair came loose from her pony tail as she thrashed against them. One man shoved her violently into the backseat of the car and the other man climbed in behind her. Before climbing into the driver's seat, the man with the leather jacket turned and looked directly at Maddy.

"Hey, you!" Through a trick of the wind, the sound carried. Maddy flinched when she heard his deep voice roar in her ear.

# CHAPTER SIX

*Y*ates trotted up the ridge, stood beside Garrick and looked down on the training field below. "What's he doing down there? We finished our morning exercises hours ago."

"He senses something." Garrick answered without taking his eye off the unicorn that galloped from one end of the expansive field to the other.

Yates' eyes went up. "Should I put out the call to the others?"

"Not yet. His intuition may be better than most but even *he* doesn't know where he will be going yet."

"But he feels something already? How is that even possible? I only feel the jolt of the incarnatus a few seconds before I get plucked away."

"You can't be surprised," he answered drily. "After all, you've trained beside him, seen him accomplish tasks no other unicorn has before him. When Silenus puts his mind to it, he is insurmountable." Garrick narrowed his eye at the field and then twisted to look at Yates. "Something's different about him."

Yates nodded in response, "I wouldn't believe it possible, but he seems even more intense. Focused. Withdrawn." His eyes veered back and forth following the warrior below.

"Silenus told me that has been working on finding a way to locate his charge faster. To find her before things get out of control."

Yates startled, snapped his head away from the field and faced Garrick. "Of course, I understand the strategy, I just never thought it was possible."

"With Silenus, anything is possible." the commander answered.

GARRICK AND YATES took one last glance at the unicorn the younger warriors considered relentless, spun around, and headed toward the rest of their unit. Below them, with ruthless determination, Silenus continued exercises that would build his stamina and hone him for battle. Because he would do anything, everything…to save the next innocent.

# CHAPTER SEVEN

*M*addy twisted her body around on the bike and sent up a silent prayer that the man was yelling at someone else. But a quick scan told her that the street was empty. She felt the hairs go up at the nape of her neck, tightened her grip on the handlebars and shot forward.

*Where am I?* she wondered.

*What direction do I go?*

The car engine came to life behind her and her breath caught. She whipped her head up and stomped down even harder on the pedals. She wanted to take a glance backward...maybe she was overreacting, maybe the car was headed in the opposite direction. But the road ahead was uneven, she couldn't turn around without hitting a pothole and launching herself over the handlebars. Instead, she maneuvered into a higher gear, and concentrated on the street ahead.

*Faster, Maddy, faster!*

*Where am I?*

The car engine hummed behind her and Maddy's fingers fumbled, slipped when she tried to upshift once more. The bike slowed, lost momentum for what seemed like an eternity. Her trembling fingers worked to adjust the lever until finally, a cog captured the chain and this time, when she pushed her foot down, she felt the speed of the bike increase.

And heard the sedan grow closer.

Maddy's lip quivered. When she couldn't stand it anymore, she twisted her head to the left. It was worse than she thought. The car with its dark windows and imposing chrome grill, were coming up on her, horrifyingly fast.

Maddy's gut clenched, she straightened her legs and rose from her seat, using her own body weight to add force to the pedals. She angled the bike slightly, raced up the next driveway and swung the bike onto the sidewalk. It was a colossal mistake. The upheavals and cracks of the aged path along with the untrimmed tree limbs impeded her further. Out of the corner of her eye, Maddy could see that the car had reached her side and was now matching her speed and providing an intimidating escort down the deserted street.

Maddy's mouth went dry. Moisture filled her eyes and when she blinked to clear her vision, hot tears coursed over her stinging cheeks. She was afraid to look into the car beside her, to see the face of the driver.

What if it was him?

The stop sign forced her to make a decision. Turning left or continuing forward gave the car the opportunity to run her down. Her safest option, her only option, was to turn right and stay on the sidewalk. Distraught, she looked for landmarks, but the houses and street names remained unfamiliar.

Maddy negotiated the bike around the corner, felt a moment of hope when the car disappeared from her peripheral gaze. But seconds later, the driver gunned the motor and swerved the car toward the curb. She held her breath, wondering if it would jump over the barrier, the six inch obstacle between her and the street. Tires scraped against the concrete, the car lurched back into its lane, resumed its role as her loathsome shadow.

When the car slowed, angled slightly to the left, Maddy knew it was going to make a sharp turn and pull into a driveway ahead of her. The sedan would cut her off or... run her down. She leaned forward over the handlebars, knew she had to cross over the entrance before the car did. A wheezy sob escaped her throat when her pant leg caught, released again. Maddy pumped her legs desperately, frantically. The car sped toward her left side and she narrowly cleared the driveway. Its tires squealed when the car withdrew and returned to the street. With the few stolen seconds of lead she had, Maddy looked around her surroundings and this time, she recognized a landmark... and heard a sound.

The pink stucco building was her aunt's favorite bakery for shortbread cookies. A memory flashed of an afternoon walk with her, the bag crinkling between them as they sampled treats and shared funny stories. *Will I ever see her again?* And then the noise again...it sounded like hoofbeats... and she craned her neck trying to find the horse.

*Please... a mounted policeman... anybody who could help me.*

Thoughts of a rescuer disappeared when the car reappeared. It swerved wildly, surging toward the curb in a endless taunting threat. Ahead, at the bakery, a dark haired man approached the back door, inserted his key and turned the handle. She tried shouting but her voice came out wheezy and too faint for him to hear. Her head dropped when the door closed behind him.

Maddy finally knew where she was. A left turn meant she would be going toward more people, busier traffic and a public park. A right turn would take her deeper into an older, neglected neighborhood. There was no option. Maddy braked sharply, watched the sedan pass by her on the left.

She jerked the handlebars, hopped the curb, landed in the street behind the car. The bike leaned precariously but she speared the ground with her foot, righted herself and pushed on.

Screeching car brakes signaled that the driver was not giving up. But Maddy was running out of energy. There were no driveways on the opposite side and she was too weak to lift the front tire over the curb. Exhausted, she swerved, remained in the narrow street and hoped she made the right decision.

The car idled in the right lane of the intersection. She watched the driver, the man in the leather jacket, twist around in his seat trying to locate her. There was nowhere to hide. At the crosswalk, she swerved up the ramp that led to the sidewalk… and felt his eyes bore into her back.

Maddy was too spent to twist her body and search for the source of the rhythmic hoofbeats that echoed in her ears again. Nor did it matter anymore. The park was still several long blocks away. Her chest hurt, she could not get enough air into her lungs and now her legs balked, refused to continue their rotations. She slowed involuntarily.

*I'm not going to make it.*

The sedan's engine roared. Resignation dropped over her. *He's going to get me.* She dropped her head, released a sob… and waited to see what he would do next.

Noises blared from behind…car brakes, a high pitched whinny, growls and curses. "Did you see that? What in the …." the words faded in the commotion but Maddy recognized the man's voice and shuddered.

A sliver of hope blossomed in her chest and she twisted in her seat. The sedan was trapped in the middle of the intersection with a lot of other cars—and a dark horse? Horns blared and angry drivers exited their cars and gestured wildly. Maddy looked ahead, considered joining a peloton of cyclists that came from her left but her legs felt swollen and heavy under her jeans. There was no way she would keep up. She took a shagged breath and set her sights ahead.

Large brass letters announced the entrance to Liberty Park and Maddy coasted through an arch flanked by fall chrysanthemums. She swung to the right, entered the parking lot where silver, black and neon clad bikers gathered for a group ride. Exhausted, she dropped her legs to the ground, slumped forward on the bike and closed her eyes.

Maddy swiped at her brow with a shaky hand when sweat trailed down her forehead and into her eyes. Heat radiated under the thick braid trailing down her back and she lifted it, shivering as the wind caressed wet strands at the nape of her neck. An occasional park goer glanced her way but saw nothing unusual in another flushed bike rider. She was air hungry and took long deep breaths despite the chilled draft that burned her throat. With reluctance, she lifted her head cautiously and looked in the direction she had come. There was no sign of the sedan. Her gaze shifted to the activities in the park.

An antique red firetruck was getting considerable attention from a horde of excited children. A large mustached fireman helped a chubby toddler into the driver's seat while his mom waved energetically through the window. One dark haired preschooler squatted to look at the underside of the truck while another older child thumped energetically on the oversized tires. Maddy squinted, looked away when the sunlight caught the panel of shiny gauges.

*I have to get out of here.*

Maddy shielded herself behind pedestrians and bikers while searching the parking lot and surrounding streets for any sign of the sedan. She wove her way through strollers, dogs and excited children until she circled the park and arrived at the entrance once again. Still no sedan.

She replaced her helmet when the cold breeze slipped through her sweater, reached her sweaty skin. *Stay on busy streets*, she told herself. Her movements were sluggish, her legs hurt, rebelled at her command to resume their rotations. But she needed to go home.

*What just happened?*

*Was that girl really being kidnapped?*

When Maddy finally turned the last corner on her way home, she saw her parents criss-crossing the driveway carrying assorted soccer equipment into the garage. Her mom finished, headed for the kitchen door but her dad caught sight of her and paused with a tilted head and surprised look. His eyebrows lifted and he smiled widely.

"You did go for that ride! That's great! Guess you're a bit tall for your own bike, hey, Maddy? Maybe we need to start looking for something bigger for you." Maddy pulled off the helmet and shrugged. She felt her face grow warm and her hands tremble as she guided the bike into the garage. Her dad took the handlebars from her, leaned the bike against the wheelbarrow and then pulled her into his chest for a hug. She wrapped her hands around his waist, savored the feeling of the heat that passed through his flannel shirt and warmed her cheeks and fingers.

"Better get you inside, sweetheart, you're practically frozen!" he joked, resting his hand at her back.

Maddy hugged him again, a bit fiercer then usual. He stilled, felt her tremors. "Hey, this is more than being a bit cold. What's going on Maddy?"

Maddy looked up at her dad with tears coursing down her face. "We have to call the police, I think I saw a kidnapping." she said.

"What? What are you talking about?"

"I saw some men and I think they were kidnapping a girl and then they chased me in the car and I was so scared…."

His arms tightened around her body. "Are you okay?"

"No, I mean…yes. I got away, but the girl didn't. I was really scared, Dad."

Her father lifted one hand, ran his fingers through his hair, frowned. "Are you sure Maddy? You don't think … maybe… that you just *thought* it was a kidnapping….are you sure the car was going to hit you? I mean this is the first time in a long while that you've gone out by yourself and…*that* must have been scary."

Maddy withdrew slightly from her dad's arms, looked up warily at the doubtful tone of his voice. "It swerved all over the street and tried to run me down."

"Was it a bunch of teenagers fooling around?"

"No, the driver looked old, like you."

"Thanks Maddy…" Her dad drew his brows together, searched her face with a expression of concern and used the hem of his flannel shirt to dab the tears from her cheeks. "Umm, maybe he was having a bad day and took it out on you. You know, like road rage?"

"But what about the girl? I think they were kidnapping her." Maddy's voice hitched on the words.

Maddy's dad paused, searched for the right words. "I just don't think it's very likely. Remember when you thought that woman was kidnapping the little boy and you asked me to stop the car and check on him…and we found out that he was mad because he was getting pulled away from his video game? Or the time you saw the neighbor's kid get into the car with the babysitter and you panicked? Maybe this girl just didn't want to go somewhere, like Tanner and the dentist? You worry too much, Maddy. What about the time you thought…"

"Okay, okay I get it." Maddy looked up into her dad's earnest eyes and *really, really* hoped he was right. She must have misunderstood what happened, somehow. It wasn't the first time *that* had happened. She stepped backward, pulled out of his arms and gave him a half-hearted smile before walking toward the kitchen door.

"I love you Maddy-girl." he called out. "I'm proud of you for going out on that ride."

"I love you too, Dad." she replied.

The wind ruffled Maddy's hair as she made her way in to the house, past leaves that skittered and slid across the driveway. Noises, both routine and reassuring, spilled out into the quiet morning when she pulled the door open. Zeus was barking for his morning treat and Tyler was yelling about a missing sweatshirt. Tanner probably took it and buried it somewhere. Again.

Maddy knew her dad was probably right. Ever since that near-abduction of her brothers, she was apprehensive, suspicious of ordinary events. But the problem was, that man was still out there and she knew there were others just like him.

# CHAPTER EIGHT

*M*addy's lab partner, Stuart, smirked as she walked into the first period science class with seconds to spare. By virtue of their last names, O'Brien and Peters, Maddy and Stuart were assigned one of the couplets of stations that ran the length of the room. Stuart was not an ideal lab partner. Fudgebuckets, she thought, clenching her teeth in preparation for his next assault. Stuart was lanky, had dirty brown hair that covered his eyes and he wore black concert teeshirts from bands she had never heard of. As far as Maddy could tell, his one goal in life was to torment her. He tripped her in the hallway, pilfered her homework papers, and pointed the finger at her after making peculiar bodily noises. Last week, he wrote profanity on her locker, which led to her receiving a slip of paper bearing an assigned appointment time with the school guidance counselor. "For heaven's sake," she had pled to the overworked woman, "it wasn't me, those words aren't even spelled correctly."

After she finished an announcement that Maddy was too preoccupied to hear, the teacher looked expectantly toward her table. Maddy had no idea what she was supposed to do but Stuart did. He stood up from his chair, flung his over-stuffed, messy backpack over his shoulder, and walked toward another desk in the rear of the room.

Maddy's teacher strolled to the door and conferred with a frizzy-haired woman for several minutes. The counselor rifled through a stack of papers, dropped several, picked them up again, finally withdrew the correct form and handed it triumphantly to the teacher. The paper was accepted, the encounter came to a close, and the teacher escorted the new student to the front of the room.

"Class, would you please welcome Allison Sheldon? Allison, would you like to tell us about yourself?"

"Thank you for welcoming me into the classroom," she began. Allison had round glasses that unfortunately emphasized her also round face. Her mousy brown hair was cut in a page boy style that landed at her chin and her outfit, a navy twin sweater set and khaki skirt, looked oddly out of place compared to the scruffy sweatshirts and jeans of the rest of the class. Allison continued her own introduction with perfectly erect posture and a brown satchel in one hand.

"As the teacher said, my name is Allison Sheldon and I recently moved from New Jersey. I have no brothers or sisters but I hope to have a cat one day. I enjoy reading fiction and riding bikes. I look forward to getting to know all of you." Puzzled expressions and narrowed eyes followed the new girl down the aisle as she walked assuredly to the vacant seat next to Maddy.

Maddy turned to look over her new partner, now sitting primly at attention in the seat beside her. Allison took off her spotless glasses to polish them on her sweater and Maddy noticed two things. Allison had stark blue eyes surrounded by long lashes, both well hidden by the dark framed glasses. And despite her serene expression, Allison's hands trembled, uncontrollably. In a move that appeared both subtle and practiced, Maddy watched her slide her arms under the desk.

AT SCHOOL THE NEXT DAY, Maddy navigated around the noisy lunch room until she spied Allison making a slow entrance into the crowded hall. Allison's expression went from hopeful to downcast as she scanned the room.

"I've been looking for you," Maddy said, ignoring the other students as they nudged each other and rolled their eyes. She took Allison by her arm and guided her to a table. "How's it going? Hopefully it's not too horrible being a new student."

Allison looked at Maddy with solemn eyes. "I'm sure that I will enjoy my experience here."

Maddy squinted her eyes in puzzlement as she replied, "Why? Why are you sure?"

Allison froze and Maddy had the oddest sensation that she had taken Allison off script.

"I think you'll have a great time Allison, it's just that you speak so grown up and it's weird."

Pink spots bloomed on Allison's cheeks and her eyes grew glassy before she averted her gaze to the side. Her fingers picked at an invisible piece of lint on her skirt.

"So, I've already decided that we're going to be friends. You might as well tell me what's going on...." Maddy took the paper napkin from her lunch bag and handed it to Allison as they both sat down. Allison dabbed her eyes and looked up to Maddy with an expression that could only be called hopeful.

"Why?"

"Why what?" Nonchalantly, Maddy unpacked her lunch. Her options had expanded since Aunt Rose moved to town and inspired her mom. Hummus, pita chips and spring peas were part of the new lunch menu offerings.

"Why did you decide you're going to be my friend?"

"You saved me from a fate worse then death, Allison. I need to warn you about Stuart... but he's the only one...everyone else is cool. Nothing to be scared about."

"Oh, I'm not scared really."

"Well, you could've fooled me." Maddy opened her hummus and offered a chip to Allison.

"It's just very important that I fit in and I'm not so good at doing that."

"Yeah, I know what you mean."

Allison's eyes lit up with interest and she leaned forward to continue. "My dad said this is a lucky opportunity to redeem myself after embarrassing them at my last school."

Maddy stilled, her hand remained in the paper bag in the act of retrieving a bottle of water. "Embarrassing them how?"

"He says I have no leadership skills, make inappropriate friends and my grades are below his expectations. My mom says I need to slim down but she said she's going to help me." She pointed at the uninspiring bag of carrots in front of her. "Still want to be my friend?" she asked tentatively in a voice that was meant to be joking but somehow fell flat.

"Of course. Try your carrots with this, you might like them better." Maddy motioned to the hummus.

Allison, Maddy learned, had a wicked sense of humor, loved stuffed animals and absolutely believed in a zombie apocalypse. Maddy told her about the scare the family had the previous summer when one of the dogs ate an entire tube of toothpaste. Allison laughed to hear the vet had expected nothing more serious than 'minty fresh poop'. Allison explained the complex color code in her school planner. Maddy giggled when she saw some of the notations like...

Thursday, 4:20pm, launch a drone to Mars to investigate living conditions.

Maddy felt a connection to Allison, thought she was different from the rest of the girls her own age. And although the two girls had fun together, laughed a lot, Maddy sensed a hint of darkness in her new friend. Knew, somehow, that Allison didn't believe the world was all giggles, milkshakes and trendy shoes.

# CHAPTER NINE

*S*ilenus trotted through the wet grass and thought about a dead girl.

That fearful glance rocked him, remained imprinted in his memory. He was starting to question his decision to protect these innocents. When he was a soldier, he expected losses, hopefully more on the enemies' side of course, but within his own squad also. It was part of warfare. When he decided to commit his life to being a protector, he never *considered* failure. The stakes are so much higher, these were children, not warriors. Their injuries….their *deaths* weighed heavy on him. He was slowly losing his mind.

And while the other unicorns accepted the consequences of the perpetual battle of good versus evil, Silenus rallied against the *wrongness* of it all. Unicorns arriving too late or, worse yet, frightening the very ones they were designed to protect. It was unacceptable, unforgivable.

Silenus had been thinking about the event that wrenched him through time toward the endangered innocent. He always assumed that fear, the adrenaline response, was what drew him to his specific charge. But a human's response to panic was universal whether it was a five year old or a seventy year old. It all felt the same to him.

Maybe the fear was the string that pulled at him but something else was the actual link. That's when he noticed that he *recognized* their voices. He wasn't sure how that was even possible. But he knew that when he arrived at a scene, all it took was a sigh, a gasp, a scream and he was able to identify her from sometimes literally thousands of others.

And so it was that Silenus spent more time studying the training field where the incarnatus occurred. He considered every tree, pondered every hill, perused the very strands of grass crushed and bent by morning exercises. But the fields and the mists that swirled and churned refused to give up their secrets.

Until one day. It was happenstance, really, that showed Silenus the way. He was galloping across the meadow one morning, changed course suddenly and burst through one of the swirling eddies of fog. And as he cut through, he heard a voice, a child's voice. From that day on, he chased the vapor, pushing through it with perked ears, he listened for their voices. Hoping for that recognition, like a key turning in a lock, that would tell him it was her. And each day he grew more anxious.

Silenus knew he needed to find a way to break through the barrier that divided the past from the present, the warrior from his charge. He needed to reach his ward and earn her trust so that he had a better chance to save her.

It was the only way he knew to save himself.

## CHAPTER TEN

*ulsa State Fair, September 2016*

THE AIR SMELLED OF POPCORN, fried foods, and sugary funnel cakes. And with every inhalation, Maddy felt bile rise to her throat from her churning stomach. She knew her dad was taking covert glances at her so she plastered a smile over her clenched teeth and told herself, *I can do this.* While Tanner and Tyler lunged at each neon flashing amusement ride promising a thrill of a lifetime, she nervously scanned the crowd. Ever since the incident with her brothers, whenever she was in a large crowd she would get nauseated and the back of her head would throb, just like it did *that* day.

*He could be here.*

She no longer voiced her concern to her parents, it only made her mother shoot worried glances at her father. And then her dad would draw her aside and try to reassure her *again.* She knew they thought she was just paranoid. But the headache and queasiness was real…and it wasn't just crowds that brought it on. Sometimes she would be in an elevator with just a few people, or walking by a cluster of people on the sidewalk, and she would be overcome with the shooting pain and a dire need to vomit. But it would pass as quickly as it came. And, over time, Maddy learned to suppress it, to manage it. But she still hated the State Fair. And so while her mom crunched on a corny dog and Tyler outlined a plan to train Zeus to be a stunt dog, she remained reserved, vigilant.

SILENUS HAD no trouble recognizing what was going on around him. Throughout the centuries, people gathered in an escape from their everyday lives, savored the same foods, laughed at jesters and cheered at competitors. No, the scene around him was not what had him astonished. It was the fact that he was here, had traveled through time, without experiencing the incarnatus. Now, he had to find her...amongst the thousands that swept all around him. His eyes darted around the crowd. A toddler being lifted onto a parent's back, couples with entwined arms and matching steps, clumps of school children.

*Was she even here?*

He stilled, his muscles taut, when he saw a girl dart and weave through the crowd. He released his breath as her friend caught up and they joined hands, continued their race. There was noise all around him. People in all directions. What if he could not find her without the incarnatus? He felt nothing. No adrenaline surges.

Nothing.

MADDY WASN'T interested in tossing colored rings over bottles for a chance to win a hot pink stuffed elephant. She stood, with her back toward her family, watching the stream of people flow through the fair grounds. Ahead of her, the crowd parted and merged again around something large. Curious, she glanced behind her, confirmed that her family remained engaged in the competition, and took a few steps in that direction.

Her skin prickled and she felt an almost physical tugging as she drew closer. Whatever it was, no one else appeared too interested. She, on the other hand, was no longer curious but *compelled*. She narrowed her eyes and tilted her head to see beyond the endless stream of people but it was no use, she was not tall enough and there were too many fairgoers. A few more steps would take her out of visual range of her family but at this point, she had no choice. For as she moved closer, it was as if layers of soft cotton encircled her, shielding her from her surroundings. The nausea lessened and the pain in the back of her head receded.

She moved faster now. She scooted past the woman with the stroller, past the teenager with earbuds, edged around the couple that stopped to debate which concession stand to try next. Until she was there.

"Whoa..." she whispered. She blinked and opened her mouth in awe.

This was no ordinary carnival animal. It was spectacular, massive, regal. It was a unicorn, pitch black with scars that slashed across his otherwise sleek hide. Its burnished gold horn blazed with reflected sunlight. Her mind hummed in bewilderment. It was as if a huge dome had been placed over the two of them. She felt normal, normal....in the midst of this huge crowd. No headache. No nausea. And despite how impressive he appeared, not one person seemed to notice the beast, their bodies shuffled sideways automatically and then returned to center.

Was it her imagination or was it staring straight at her?

She felt oddly drawn but leapt back in fear, nonetheless, when the unicorn suddenly flung his head backward, stomped on the ground and exhaled loudly.

"It's you." She heard his voice, deep and resonant, as she swiveled and pushed through the crowd. She felt the odd awareness, the familiarity, fade as she drew further away. Maddy winced, pinched the bridge of her nose and took a deep breath when the pain returned. The tap on the shoulder startled her and she swung wildly.

"I found her!" Tyler shouted. His twin appeared behind Tyler's shoulder, followed by her parents on her opposite side. Her mom reached out and hugged her, worry written on her face, but her dad held back and tilted his head as he examined her.

He finally came forward, held up her chin and looked into her eyes. "We got separated and you did okay. You didn't panic. We got separated and nothing happened." Maddy nodded back to him and he drew her into a bear hug.

Maddy turned to look over her shoulder, toward the direction she had come from. Her dad was wrong, something *had* happened.

# CHAPTER ELEVEN

*M* *idtown Tulsa, October 2016*

Rose chewed on her bottom lip as she swiped at the glass and concentrated on getting the last streaks removed. Stenciled gold letters were applied yesterday to the front window and now *The Last Chapter* was almost ready to open. She leaned back, rag in hand, and looked with pride at her work. Staring back her, through the window was a small boy, surely no older than seven. Rose opened the door and peered down at him.

"I would like to look at the books about fire trucks," the boy requested.

"We haven't opened yet," Rose explained.

"That's ok, I'll just be looking" he countered, looking up to her expectantly.

Rose opened the door wider, looked down the street for a parent, shrugged her shoulders and let the young boy in. His hair needed a good comb and she suspected the rain boots were in homage to firemen and not because precipitation was expected. She directed him to the children's section and started working on removing the layer of dust that new construction always leaves behind. "What's your name, honey?"

"TJ, and I was really hoping for a reference book on fire trucks." he requested patiently.

*What an odd little bird,* she thought.

She walked down a few aisles. "I really don't know if I have any books specifically on fire trucks, I don't remember unpacking anything, perhaps George...." Rose continued to walk, fingers brushing the spines of the books as she looked over them.

"I found one! Modern Fire Truck: An Illustrated History," TJ called out excitedly.

George walked into the shop with a bag of bagels and twin cups of coffee. "Who's the little one?" he asked, pointing his chin toward the sole occupant of the wooden table.

"I found TJ out front," she whispered. "He's especially fond of fire truck books, but not the children's version." she whispered.

George looked over the coffee cup at the young boy. "I believe I'll introduce myself."

Rose took the bagels and coffee to the back room, soon to be their break room. She sipped on the coffee and made a small grimace. Coffee was okay but she preferred tea. It doesn't matter, she told herself. I will have this room set up in no time. She opened up the first box and got to work, excited to tackle another area of the shop. She felt her back tighten up a bit and mentally added a soak in the bathtub to her list of things to do.

Hours later, Rose heard the door chime and called out, "George, I think we should take a break and grab some lunch". She looked up to see a teenager standing in front of her instead of George. Wary and frayed, Rose noted. She put a hand to her back, pulled herself up from the partially unloaded box and addressed the teenager.

"I'm sorry, we aren't quite open yet."

"I'm looking for a job," the girl replied with downcast eyes.

Rose looked her over thoughtfully. "I need some tea," she said, "would you join me? My name is Rose, by the way, but most people call me Aunt Rose. Do you take milk in your tea? Do you drink tea?" Rose removed some invoices from the stool and motioned toward it.

"I guess most people drink coffee but that just seems a bit *abrupt* for some mornings, don't you agree?" she continued. "It's getting close to lunch time but a little biscotti won't hurt us any? Right? I'm pretty sure I have some around here somewhere." Rose scratched her head, leaned over and rummaged through an open box. "By the way, what did you say your name was?"

"Sloane... and... tea is fine."

Minutes later, Rose poured the hot water over the strainers and waited for the tea to steep. As the steam rose from the china cups, Rose glanced over at young teenager. Sloane's clothing, while clean, was an odd assortment. Or maybe the current fashion? Rose admitted to herself that she really had no clue on teenage fashion. Sloane's top was oversized and her skirt... Well never mind, she thought, I would love to be able wear short skirts again. Sloane's hair was put up in a likely attempt to make her look older but the escaping wisps only served to make her look more waif-like.

She looks so frail, Rose thought. She swirled a spoon briefly and held the cup out. Sloane nervously accepted. She held the rose patterned cup and saucer gingerly in her hands, her face a mixture of confusion and stoic determination. "Don't worry about the china, honey, I collect these cups in garage sales and people love to help me find them...they all have roses on them you might notice."

Rose took surreptitious glances at the teenager as they chatted. Sloane sat ramrod straight with her hands gripped in her lap. She had given up on the teacup, placed it on the countertop behind her, when she couldn't stop the clattering of the cup in the saucer. Rose took another sip, placed her cup on the counter beside Sloane's. "Now, tell me what type of job you're looking for…"

Rose was rinsing the dishes in soapy water when George returned. "I think we need an employee," Rose said.

"What? We don't need any help. We finally have the shop ready to open. What in the world are you talking about?" George would have gotten frustrated and possibly angry in earlier times but years with Rose taught him to roll with the changes. Or get *swallowed* by the tidal wave...he looked up, resigned to what was ahead.

Rose outlined the plan. Neither George nor Rose had a lot of internet experience and one goal was, of course, to sell the books online. She and Sloane had discussed keeping inventory of the books and starting online sales as soon as possible. She suspected that Sloane had no idea how to do this but she did appear confident with her computer skills so Rose knew they would figure it out, eventually.

Rose followed up with a description of Sloane. Sloane really need this job, she explained. George grunted. He'd never been convinced that the used bookstore was going to be a sound financial plan in the first place. He mentally moved it from the category of post retirement income to community service.

Rose was making progress after her interruptions earlier that morning. She looked up at George when she heard an odd noise. "Did you hear that? George! Did you hear that noise?"

"What, no… What noise?"

Rose considered, once again, the possibility that George had lost some of his hearing due to the numerous rock concerts that he attended. It might also be the volume of music he listened to in the car, when he was alone in the shop….

George looked at Rose and sensed a lecture coming.

"I'll go investigate," he said as he escaped toward the back office. As he reached the back of the shop he could hear the noise, a pounding on the back door. He opened the door and looked down at his niece.

"My favorite niece! Come in, Madison," he said opening the door wider. "Rose has been looking forward to showing you the bookstore. We're just about to wrap it up for the day."

Maddy, to everyone except her uncle George, propped her bike against the brick wall in the alley and made her way into the warm book store. She dropped her backpack on the floor as she stepped over the threshold. Rose met her at the door, enveloped Maddy in her arms and then spun her forward and guided her into the shop.

"Welcome to The Last Chapter, Maddy!"

Maddy looked around at the cozy shop and back at her aunt. Rose was beaming with pride. The aged wood floors had been sanded and lightly stained during the renovation, the remaining scars giving testimony to their age. Industrial lighting had been replaced with vintage school house lights and cushy arm chairs were positioned in reading nooks. It was perfect.

The back room, now break room, had a shelf of unstained pine that ran the distance of the narrow room. Dainty rose adorned cups mixed in with thick mugs. Canisters labeled with Rose's favorite teas - *There will be Blood Orange, Gaucho Grey and Texas Chili Chai* stood next to baskets of hot cocoa mix. A final mug announcing "Coffee is not my cup of Tea" was loaded with mismatched spoons. Stools provided seats if you could navigate around the unopened boxes.

Maddy hugged Rose and George spontaneously. "I love it! Everyone will love it!"

George dug deep into his pocket and pulled out a brass key. "Rose and I wanted you to have a key to our shop. We want you to feel welcome here. Be careful and don't lose it though."

"Oh, George, of course she won't lose it."

Maddy took the key and held it in her hand. Funny how something so small could mean something really big.

"Maddy, we're going to run down the street and get some dinner, why don't you join us?"

"Oh, I'd love to but I have to head home and study. I just stopped by to see the shop."

Rose squeezed Maddy before grabbing her purse and calling out for George. "Ok, call your mother if you are going to stay a bit, otherwise, be careful on the road, dear."

Maddy watched her aunt and uncle through the window as they strolled down the street toward the Italian restaurant. She stood still, breathing in the smells of the bookshop. The musty smell of the older books mixed with the varnish and pine scented cleaners. A lavender candle still burned by checkout counter. Maddy blew out the flame and pictured George shaking his head in resignation at Aunt Rose. *For heaven's sake Rose, it's a bookshop. Do you want to start a fire?* Maddy spent a moment watching the smoke curl upward before turning around to do a closer inspection of the store.

She glanced at the various categories and then paused to examine the Moroccan cookbooks, one of Rose's new interests. Spying a favorite mystery author she grabbed a book and fell into the orange club chair. Propping her feet up, she peered over the spine of the book, taking in the creamy walls and pine shelves. It really was quite perfect. Maddy rose again, a small smile on her face. She carefully returned the book to the shelf and spun around, once more, to look over the shop. It took a few minutes to locate the right light switch and then she headed toward the back door, her thoughts now on tomorrow's history test.

Maddy turned to pull the heavy steel door shut. Satisfied with the click as the lock engaged, she turned around to leave. And stopped. Standing in front of her, in the back alley, was the unicorn. From the State Fair.

It stood motionless with one foreleg advanced and its head bent forward. Its eyes were closed and its burnished gold horn was close enough she could reach out and touch it with her finger if she wanted. And she did want to…for some reason, she felt curiously pulled to the creature. But very, very frightened of it too.

Maddy was transfixed for a second, but then reacted. She moved her backpack toward her chest to act as a shield. Seeing no movement from the large animal, she reversed course and flung it on her back again as she sprang sideways and dashed past it. Desperately hoping the backpack might protect her from being impaled, she ran.

In a deep voice that had to be her frightened imagination, she heard the unicorn behind her proclaim, "By my sacred Oath and until my dying breath, I pledge to protect you, Madison."

# CHAPTER TWELVE

*S*ilenus turned his head, watched another frightened girl run away from him. She disappeared around the corner and he was left alone, remembering how it all began...

Silenus' hooves bit into the rocky soil leaving a cloud of dust behind as he surged up the final hill. The ascent was steep. But the blood that hammered through his veins was not from the meager exertion required for the incline, it was leftover adrenaline that still coursed through his body. He took deep breaths of the pine-scented air, savored the slight burn of his muscles. Oftentimes, he had stumbled up this same hill, bloodied and weary. Today, he soared. He whinnied, heard the response of fellow unicorns as they made the final push toward home.

By this time, the families would be gathering and climbing this same rise to meet the soldiers at the crest. His wife's intuition unerringly predicted when he was returning home and she would gather his daughter Flora, and greet him on his arrival. Flora would nuzzle and rub against his wife and then prance up and down the hill as they waited with the others. Once home, Silenus would tickle his daughter's muzzle with his coarse whiskers and watch her eyes sparkle and her snowy white tail flick back and forth. Flora would playfully side-step away from him before returning to slide under his neck and stretch out her head, her soft mane tickling his chin with her caresses.

Warriors called out in neighs and whinnies to their loved ones on the opposite side of the hill, and Silenus' ears pricked up as he listened for their responses. He would know his wife's soft nicker, the sound that greeted him each morning when she tenderly touched his muzzle and they breathed in the scent of each other. And though this absence was shorter than most, he relished the homecoming that awaited him.

Upon Garrick's signal, the ranks dissolved and the warriors raced each other to the top of the hill, eager for their reunions. Garrick reached the crest first and halted with such ferocity that Silenus wondered if he was trying to avoid some errant unicorn child. Moments later, the entire unit came to a halt, forming a sweeping line behind their leader. The morning mist was beginning to disperse, allowing glimpses of the desecration below. Silenus' breath caught in his chest.

Shredded hides. Mangled limbs. Blood…and more blood.

Ear-piercing squeals and furious snorts broke the silence around Silenus. With narrowed, fierce eyes, he rose up on massive hind legs, flattened his ears and roared. Dust and rubble spit in all directions as his forelegs slammed back into the earth. He lowered his head, pointed his horn toward a scene more dreadful than any battle he had ever faced, and charged.

Silenus slowed as he came upon the first bodies. As a seasoned warrior, he was no stranger to blood and mayhem but this slaughter of innocence rattled him. He grimly examined each body with tumultuous emotions, sorrowful when he recognized other's wives and children but with rising hope when he failed to find his own.

Garrick stayed motionless at the top of the hill. His unit wove among the bodies with various reactions to the slaughter. Cedric retreated to the periphery of the field after descending the hill, unable to move further, while Aldrich bolted feverishly amongst the bodies. Yates was the first to identify his wife and now stumbled like a drunk over the flayed legs of the dead.

Awareness settled into Silenus. An odd thing had happened in the skirmish earlier that morning, an event he had never witnessed in all his previous battles. Soon after the fighting had begun, the enemy swiftly disengaged and departed in a mass exodus through the trees. Now Silenus knew why. The battle was a diversion, and the result of their failure to recognize this strategy lay in the carnage before him. The families had been the true target.

Silenus shoved emotion down and boldly, systematically, scrutinized the victims strewn throughout the meadow. He saved the copse of trees for last. Coming down the hill, he'd determined that tactically, the trees provided the best defensive position. It would be the only logical place to go if you had a younger, slower unicorn to protect. It was there, under a canopy of graceful tree limbs and flickering sunlight that he found them both. He knew his wife, who was known for her speed, gave up any chance of escape in order to shield their beloved daughter. She was bloodied, her chest splayed open, her pearly horn crimson stained. His daughter looked peaceful, undefiled with the exception of a single puncture wound to the chest. Her tiny horn sparkled as it caught rays of sun filtering through the trees.

Silenus nuzzled his wife, but although her body was still warm, she remained motionless. He leaned down to breath in her essence but instead the metallic scent of blood hit his nose. Tears slid down his muzzle and dropped in dark splotches on both his wife and daughter. Tears that would normally heal wounds and cure poisons but were ineffective against death. He pawed at the ground in front of them, sending up dust that cloaked his mouth and burned his eyes.

Looking up through a film of grief, Silenus saw a solitary figure in the middle of the field and realized it was Garrick. Unicorns, looking for answers and solace, began gathering around their leader. Silenus closed his eyes, took a deep breath and turned away from his loved ones to slowly trot toward the herd of soldiers. He overheard Garrick talking to Egorn, one of the younger unicorns as they stood in front of the mutilated remains of Egorn's mother and sister. "They died quickly with no pain," Garrick gruffly declared.

Silenus met the eyes of the older warrior and knew he lied.

Garrick's ears pricked up at a commotion in the distance. He tossed his head, snorted coarsely and the unicorns fell back into formation at his command, testimony to his leadership and their training despite the devastation around them. In tight ranks, their heads rose in unison to watch the townspeople descend into the valley.

The path between the valley and the town was well worn by both boot and hoof. Just as the unicorns could be relied on to heal any pestilence in the village, the humans traditionally attended to the injured warriors after battle. Over the ridge, a few heads bobbed into sight, then a wall of humans cascaded down the incline. Some of the older boys separated from the group and raced down the hill, their bare feet flying through the dewy meadow grass.

Warriors, in dark hues of gray, black and brown, stood as a unit in the center of the clearing while their gentle unicorn counterparts, their snowy hides slashed and torn, lay in unnatural positions encircling them.

For the second time that day, the unicorns were witness to the slaughter of innocence as the boys recognized the victims and reacted. Some stepped backward, their eyes anxiously seeking out the faces of their own mothers and sisters. Others fell to their knees gagging and retching. The women hurried forward to reach the boys, dropping useless baskets filled with dressings and liniments intended for the wounded. They collected the younger children, cupped hands over their eyes or shoved them behind skirts to shield them from the massacre before them. Pitchfork-bearing men took up the rear, fanning out behind the women and children, they uneasily scanned the hills for any signs of the attackers.

Silenus' gaze darted amongst the townspeople, both consoled and agitated when it finally landed on one particular child. Clara. The girl's face was pale, her eyes wide with worry. When she caught sight of him, she pulled out of her mom's grasp and wove through the throng to stand in front of him.

"Where is she, where's Flora?" she pleaded.

Silenus dropped his head, unsure how to answer his daughter's best friend. Clara's mother caught up with her daughter, laid a protective hand on her shoulder and looked over her head to meet Silenus' gaze. Silenus motioned his head toward the grove where his loved ones lay.

The younger warriors criss-crossed the fields charging invisible foes while snorting and thrashing their heads. Their horns flashed in the morning sunshine when they shook their heads and reared up. The older unicorns stood by silently, some heads swiveling to watch the angry youth gallop while others dipped their muzzles in defeat.

Meanwhile, the townspeople paid homage to the dead. Women used cloths dipped in the nearby stream to rinse the blood away from both horns and hides. It was an impossible task. While the stream darkened with the blood of the fallen, the women continued their toil, seeking to erase the evidence of the annihilation. Exhausted and seeing the futility, one by one they gave up, oftentimes falling to their knees with hands clutching familiar manes.

Silenus glanced to the grove where he saw Clara kneeling over his daughter's body. The bottom of her dress was smudged with mud and another streak of dirt marred her cheek. Clara's mom pulled a lavender ribbon from her daughter's hair and together they braided it in Flora's once snowy mane. Finishing, Clara slumped forward and nestled in the curve of his daughter's neck.

Men gathered fire wood for the funeral pyres. Sheer size and numbers of the fallen unicorns made burial impossible. A dozen fires were started in the meadow and they burned through the day and well into the night. The townspeople stayed as the sun went down and stars emerged like glowing embers that had swelled into the heavens. Husbands wrapped their arms around their wives and stared into the dancing flames wondering the fate of the unicorn warriors. Unicorns mated for life and lived forever, *unless* pierced in the heart. In a few hours, the future of the unicorn race had been obliterated.

Silenus listened as high-pitched voices rose up over the crackling of the fires and humming conversations of the townspeople. The younger warriors were talking of revenge. One unicorn stomped his hoof emphatically while another violently bolted away from the group, weaving between the people and fires, only to return later and resume the terse exchange. Garrick's voice could be heard trying to quell the angry unicorns. As usual, he encouraged them to formulate a plan for revenge instead of rushing out in a fit of bloodlust.

"You must separate your pain and lock it away," he warned.

Silenus dropped his head, depleted, desolate. The clamor of the angry unicorns was deafening but Silenus heard nothing.

Clara's dad strode across the field as he heard the mounting turbulence. He drew both Clara and his wife to his chest and looked over at the angry warriors. He had no real fear of the unicorns as the friendship with their kind had been for generations. But some of the warriors were thrashing and stomping and he worried that one of the children would be accidentally injured. He gathered his family, prepared for the walk home in the dark.

Silenus looked up and recognized their plans for departure. The fire reflected off Clara's golden curls and her tears shimmered in streams down her cheeks. Her father leaned down, absentmindedly placed a kiss on the top of her head as he urged her away from the fire. Silenus stepped in front of the family and nickered softly. Clara's dad knit his brow and looked toward his daughter for an explanation, children were far better at communicating with the unicorns.

"He's asking permission to be my protector."

Clara's dad cocked his head and rubbed his bearded chin. Unicorns and humans had been helping each other as far back as he could remember but he had never heard of a unicorn making a request like this.

Nodding, he came to a decision. "Tell him that your mother and I would be honored to accept."

Silenus extended one hoof forward, bent the other and lowered himself into a kneeling position before the family. He closed his eyes and bowed his head down until his horn hovered slightly above the dusty earth. As if pulled by an invisible thread, Clara separated from her family, walked closer toward the massive animal, and gingerly touched the golden horn. The noise of the crowd faded away and both unicorns and humans gathered around the pair, drawn to the curiosity. Yates was the next unicorn to present himself to a human girl and then others followed suit, each lowering their horn in an ultimate act of humility. Young girls would gently touch the horns of the formidable warriors and oftentimes fling their arms around their corded and thick necks afterwards.

In the days that followed, there were two reactions to the massacre.

Most of the unicorns joined with Aldrich and plotted for revenge. They banded together and scoured the countryside searching and oftentimes finding the enemy that had destroyed their homes and family. They were ruthless.

The remaining unicorns recognized that revenge would not be a strong enough force to reconcile their indescribable grief. They swore, instead, to fiercely protect the remaining virtuous in the world.

FOR CENTURIES, Silenus kept the Oath he made that day. But one question continued to plague him…how do you protect an innocent who's afraid of you?

# CHAPTER THIRTEEN

*M*addy bolted down the alley, ignoring the stitch in her side, until she reached the end of the row of shops. She turned the corner, stopped behind the brick wall, leaned over with her hands on her knees and panted. A quick glance down the alley reassured her that she was not being followed but also reminded her of the forgotten bike.

*No way.*

The walk home was slow and uneventful and spent alternating between trying to rationalize what just happened and apprehensive peeps over her shoulder. Porch lights popped on, illuminating front entries and throwing long shadows of tangled tree limbs over the street. She brushed stands of hair from her face when the breeze picked up and mindlessly kicked at the swirling leaves at her feet. The air smelled of wood smoke as families made their way home from schools and jobs and gathered around hearths seeking a bit of warmth and comfort against the cooler nights.

The usual clamor greeted her when she arrived home, the boys were arguing about a homework assignment, Thor was whining by the pantry where the dog food was stored and her mom was reminding everyone, *for the last time*, to pick up their shoes and backpacks from the kitchen floor and put them where they belong. Her dad threw her an absent-minded smile from the kitchen table and then bent over his laptop to answer a few more emails before dinner.

"I think I saw a unicorn," Maddy blurted as she entered the warmth of the kitchen. Not surprisingly, there was no response. "I think I saw a unicorn!" Maddy's voice rose higher, insistent and tight.

Her dad finally looked up, eyebrows knit together. "What did you say?"

Tyler blandly repeated her announcement as he slung his backpack over his shoulder. "She thinks she saw a unicorn, Dad." He finished picking up his shoes, passed through the kitchen and exited the room.

"Hmm, that's very interesting dear, now wash up and get ready for dinner," said her mom. Emily scooped up plates of spaghetti and the smell of onions and garlic wafted through the kitchen.

"Can you describe it, Maddy? Because unicorns don't exist, so you likely saw a horse. Or a rhinoceros. Were you at the zoo?" Tanner appeared to be the only one listening now that the food was on the table.

"Never mind, it was *not* a rhinoceros." Maddy wanted to stomp her feet and demand attention from her family. Instead, she went to the small powder room and frowned at herself as she washed her hands to get ready for dinner.

LATER THAT EVENING Maddy's dad stared, unseeing, into his reflection as he finished brushing his teeth. His brown hair was still tousled from his evening walk with the dogs and he had yet to take off his favorite flannel shirt in preparation for bed. He removed the toothbrush from his mouth and threw his wife a frothy grin in the mirror when he felt cold hands circle his waist.

"I'm worried about Maddy," he said

"What do you mean?"

"Well, she hasn't said anything about kidnapping lately but now she's claiming that she saw a unicorn. Is this some puberty thing I should know about? Or, could it be more serious..."

Emily peeked around Dave's shoulder to meet his eyes in the mirror. Soft auburn curls framed her face and tickled his arm. "It's probably nothing." She narrowed her eyes as she reflected on his comment.

"Let's keep an eye on her, maybe she needs more of our attention. I do feel like we spend a lot of time chasing the boys around. Maybe things are rougher on her than we realize. I'll ask Rose to keep an eye on her too and let us know if she notices anything."

"What in the world is that noise?" Dave's voice croaked as he wiped the rest of the toothpaste from around his mouth.

"Basketball," Emily answered.

"No way, we talked about that."

Emily smirked at him and then scrambled into bed. She was throwing the covers over her legs when they both heard another thud from the room beyond. "Your turn." She grinned as she pointed at the door. Dave rinsed his toothbrush, turned off the bathroom light and headed toward the hallway.

# CHAPTER FOURTEEN

"*T*J, is that you?" Aunt Rose rubbed her eyes as she scurried down the aisle to unlock the front door of the shop. TJ waited patiently in the dark and then slid in when she opened the door.

"But TJ, it's quite early and I've not had my tea yet. The shop is not even open..." The wind blew a few leaves in with TJ and she watched them swirl around the shop and settle underneath some of the shelves as he entered, acting like this was his second home.

"That's ok, I'll just look at more books on firetrucks, please."

"But where's your mom? Won't someone be worried about you?"

Rose walked with him to the back room and watched him climb on a stool as she rummaged for a packet of hot cocoa. Chai tea was her morning tradition so she prepared her own cup while trying to figure out what to do with TJ.

"Mom cannot take me to school in the morning because she has to be at work early so she drops me off at my aunt's house. Aunt Luna works late at night so I'm supposed to be quiet until seven when she'll make me breakfast. Sometimes she works really late and forgets to wake up, even when I tell her." TJ motioned to the man's watch on his slender wrist. "Aunt Luna doesn't know anything about fire engines. Did the new book on the history of fire fighting equipment arrive yet?"

Rose stirred his hot chocolate, wondering if she should pick up some marshmallows at the store. "No, not yet but I expect it any day..."

Rose turned as the heavy back door opened. George stepped over the threshold and automatically flipped on the switch starting the music. Today was rock-n-roll since they'd listened to the classical music his wife preferred yesterday. It was a fair arrangement although somewhat disconcerting for the customers.

"TJ is joining us this morning," she announced.

George looked up, a bit surprised to see the young boy. "Are we still on for Saturday? As long as there are no house fires, we have a date to see the fire station."

"I'm bringing my pad to take notes. I hope to see what the average water pressure is in the hoses. I have called the city water department but the lady did not know the answer." TJ shook his head in disappointment.

"I suppose not," answered George stroking his chin, "Well, I was going to take a picture or two while we're there."

SLOANE WAS BECOMING A TEA DRINKER. She wanted to please Rose of course, but it went beyond that. With each sip from the delicate china she could feel layers of the shields she had constructed peel off. It was true that she had preferred coffee in the past, thinking tea was weak in comparison. The coffee, usually from cheap styrofoam cups, was always potent and bitter. The tea, she was learning, was more complex than she realized.

Sloane watched the steam climb upward and the tea leaves unfurl. The caramel color expanded, replaced the colorless liquid and she frowned as she waited the three minutes Rose insisted was necessary for brewing. When she finally drew the cup upward and took a sip, her thoughts were on her mother. For fourteen years she had traveled the country with her. *Wanderlust*, Simon told her. Such an interesting, almost pretty word for upheaval.

Simon, an attendant at a gas station three towns....or four?....ago explained that some people could never get comfortable in one place. They always heard the siren call of a brighter future somewhere out there. Sloane no longer bothered to listen to her mom as she described the virtues of each new destination. Instead, she numbly loaded the car with their scant possessions, put in her earbuds and pulled her hoodie over her head.

But now, Sloane was slowly unwinding from the tension that had built up over the years. And she was thinking about her future. Getting a job at The Last Chapter was the first important step in her desire to take control of her own life. Her mom was getting that antsy look she typically had before declaring it was time to move on but Sloane had no intention of leaving this time. George and Rose were kind, the shop felt cozily familiar, and yesterday she felt a pleasant buzzing in her head when a previous shopper not only recognized her but also remembered her name. It was as if invisible, slender roots were stretching from her body, curling around the pine bookshelves and anchoring her to this place. She wasn't going anywhere, somehow, she would find a way to stay.

Sloane put down her teacup and used a small key to unlock the bottom drawer of the filing cabinet behind the checkout counter where she kept her cosmetic case. The key was left out for her a few days ago along with a note from Rose, *in case you want to lock up your purse or anything else.* It was proof of her belonging, another gossamer strand tying her to the shop. She withdrew the case, carried it to the minuscule bathroom, lined the contents up along the sides of the sink and got to work. Once she was satisfied with her makeup, she reached for a brush and elastic tie to tackle her dark blonde hair.

When finished, she examined herself critically in the mirror. The black v-neck sweater with dark jeans was more conservative than her usual apparel but she believed that it fulfilled her plan to look more mature. Satisfied with her appearance, Sloane stuck her head into the back room to see what task Rose would like started.

Rose squealed in excitement. "You have blue hair!"

"Just the tips" said Sloane touching her hair nervously. "I thought I tucked them all in."

"Did you use Kool-aid?" Rose fingered the wispy colored strands, "And why are you trying to hide them?"

Sloane looked up puzzled. "Blue hair doesn't bother you?"

"Of course not. George is playing 80's music today." she said, as if this explained her views on hair color.

## CHAPTER FIFTEEN

*M*addy stood in the garage, backpack slung over one shoulder, and stared at the spot where the bike should be. A moment later she remembered everything.

*A unicorn?*

She considered her options. She could either walk to school this morning, avoiding the bookstore entirely, and explain to her mom why her bike was missing. *Ugh.* Or she could return to the bookstore, hope the unicorn was gone and that her mom's bike had not been stolen. *I mean, really,* she thought, *how long would a unicorn hang out in a back alley anyway. An imaginary unicorn, that is.*

Maddy slipped on her hat and gloves, closed the garage door and started the walk back to the bookstore. Her thoughts were not surprisingly, on unicorns. Last night she snuck out the laptop after she was supposed to be asleep and did a little Wikipedia reading on the mythical animals. Unicorns were described in many different cultures and countries including Greece, India, Ethiopia, France and Germany. Maddy was shocked to see there were even references in the Bible, well, the King James version anyway...apparently, the more recent version changed the translation to wild ox.

While they were typically thought to be white, designs on shields and flags from medieval times also depicted darker colors. Numerous accounts spoke of how difficult they were to capture. Nothing, however, explained why she saw a unicorn behind her aunt's bookshop.

*It makes no sense.*

Maddy pinched the bridge of her nose when she felt the twinge of pain, failed to notice the sedan that slid up on her left.

"Excuse me?" a familiar voice asked.

She peered into the car, confirming what she already knew. It was him, the man in the leather jacket. Their eyes met. He recognized her, she could tell by the mocking smile on his face. She turned on her heel and ran.

Cherry street was just ahead but she was afraid to stay on the side walk. She cut right, into the church parking lot, saw the back door of the sanctuary but didn't trust it to be unlocked this early in the morning. She flew past it, heard a car turn the corner into the lot behind her. The passage way between the church and the strip center was narrow, too tight for a car, so she took a sharp left turn. And froze.

The unicorn blocked her escape. His eyes were fierce and puffs of smoke shot from his flared nostrils with each exhalation. He was broad shouldered, commanding...intimidating... and with the exception of a slight quiver in his flank, he stood stationary, watching her with steely eyes. She felt her heartbeat ratchet up another level as she faced the terrifying beast. Stepped backwards. Jumped when she heard the car door slam behind her. Making a quick, desperate decision, she bolted.

"Get behind me, Madison." The unicorn's voice was

deceptively calm, at odds with the tight restraint with which he held his body. She ran past him, spun in place, and together they watched a long shadow approach the passageway.

A woman wearing a thick green cardigan turned the corner, juggling her car keys, a box of donuts and her coffee cup. Maddy closed her eyes, sagged against the side of the animal and then stiffened up when she realized what she was doing.

The unicorn curved his neck backwards. "Are you alright?"

"I'm fine...thanks," she stammered. The woman paused and threw a curious look at Maddy, who smiled weakly back at her. After balancing her coffee on the donut box, the woman pulled open the glass door and stepped inside. The door closed without a noise.

Now it was just Maddy and a unicorn...Now what?

One moment passed and then another. "What are you doing here?" she finally said.

"I'm here to protect you."

Maddy could not see any movement of the unicorn's mouth so she assumed it was some sort of telepathy that allowed their communication. It wasn't so far-fetched when you considered that a *unicorn* was standing in front of her.

"I'm okay, so you can just return to wherever you came from." Maddy spun around and continued through the passage way. The hollow clopping of hoofbeats against the pavement warned her that the unicorn had no intention of departing. She whirled around and faced him.

"Ok, who are you and what's going on? Are you real or some figment of my imagination? Am I going crazy?"

"I am Silenus. It is my duty to keep you safe."

"Silenus is a nice name, I've never heard it before." Maddy's voice cracked as she went on. She glanced over her shoulder, judging the distance to the street and possible safety. "Now please tell me why you're here and what's going on..."

Silenus was silent for a moment, and Maddy heard no other sound in the world except the steady thump of hooves as they struck the concrete pavement beside her. And then, in a voice that was deep, powerful and resonant, he began his explanation.

"A long time ago, I was part of a company of warrior unicorns. In my village, males started training as combatants soon after birth and continued until their death. Military tactics and strategies were passed from elder to youth. Older soldiers pressed the younger to build their stamina and strength and as the male unicorn's horn grew, they were taught to wield it in mock duels."

Silenus slowed and Maddy glanced up at him but his eyes were unfocused and stared out into the shadowy alley. Eventually he shook his head slightly, increased his pace again, and continued.

"I was told that I had a natural talent, one that had the elders whispering about the ancient warriors of the past. They pushed me relentlessly, working me harder than the others, and I rose to each challenge and went beyond their expectations. Garrick, the commander in charge, appointed me as his lieutenant, passing by other older and more experienced warriors. Mentally, physically, our warriors were the strongest we had ever been. We were always victorious in battle."

He paused longer this time and Maddy knew something terrible was coming, something that caused his strong, confident voice to stutter with some unnamed emotion.

"But once....*once* we failed to recognize a simple diversionary strategy and while our entire company was away at battle, they slaughtered my entire village."

Maddy stopped walking and turned to look up at the unicorn. His eyes met hers briefly and she flinched at the swirling pain before he dropped his gaze and continued talking.

"I found I was no longer interested in the pursuit of warfare. Instead, I pledged my honor, strength and devotion toward the protection of a human maiden, a young girl that was a friend to my daughter. Time passed and I continued to make new bonds with with young maidens; my Oath has remained unbroken through generations and centuries."

Maddy pursed her lips in thought. "Centuries?"

"Yes, milady, I have been in service protecting young maidens for centuries."

"Wait a minute, your entire village was slaughtered....Did your daughter die? Did your wife die?" Maddy blurted out and then immediately closed her eyes and scrunched up her face. *When will she learn to think before speaking?*

"With the exception of my unit of soldiers, I lost everyone."

Maddy looked up at the unicorn through teary eyes. "But how is it that they could die and you have not? And how have you been able to go on?"

"Unicorns can live forever but they can also be killed. I have been fortunate at avoiding that particular fate."

Maddy looked closer at Silenus and noted the numerous scars, dark slashes interrupting his glistening black hide.

"I'm glad you're alive but I'm still not sure why you're here with me." Maddy reached out with a tentative hand to touch Silenus but withdrew it, unsure whether it was acceptable to comfort a warrior unicorn.

"I'm here as your protector."

"But, I don't need a protector....do I?" Maddy's voice hitched at the end of her question and her mind whirled with the possibilities. *A unicorn appeared out of nowhere saying that she needed a protector...What was going on?*

"Maddy, I'm not sure what the future brings but I do know that you are arriving at a crossroads and you will have to pick a path. One of those roads leads to danger. I will protect you *if* you choose that direction," he answered simply.

Maddy's mouth fell open, she blinked. "Okayyy...why me?" Maddy watched a few cars pass in front of her, waited for his response.

"I can't tell exactly why I am bonded with certain maidens except to say that they have all been very unique."

Maddy looked down at her windbreaker and jeans in puzzlement. The only thing that made her unique was the phobia she could not seem to conquer. *What if her dad was right, if that 'kidnapping' she'd witnessed really was a family squabble. And today that same man was just asking directions? How strange she must've looked running away...* "I don't know what you mean."

"Nor do I have the answer for you. But I know you to be courageous. You're a warrior like me."

Maddy looked up in astonishment. Silenus was massive. Clydesdale-size massive. His burnished gold horn flashed with the last rays of the sunset, reminding her of a raised sword. Beside him she felt quite little.

"What do you mean?"

"Being a warrior is about being bold, Maddy. One has only to look at your scar to see evidence of your bravery."

Maddy's hand went self-consciously to her chin. Tucked under her chin ran an almost invisible thin white line trailing her jawline. She rubbed the area, the sensation still not normal years after the torn skin had been repaired.

"You could have run for help. Most would have. And they would have been too late."

"She saved us," she told Silenus, "the woman with the hose saved us."

"No, Madison, she saved you. You saved the twins."

"I should have been closer, I didn't even want to be with them!" Maddy looked up searching his eyes for signs of recrimination. "If I had been closer to them, that whole thing would've never happened. It was all my fault!"

"No, Madison. It was not your fault, just as it was not my fault that my family was taken from me. There will always be evil in the world and you must not take responsibility when the blame lies elsewhere." He spoke sternly and Maddy hugged herself, more from the emotion of the moment than the actual cold.

"Your actions that day revealed the heart of a warrior. You put the safety of your brothers above your own, Maddy. You did it automatically, without thought. You will need that bravery in the coming days."

Maddy's cheeks bloomed with color and she looked away as he spoke. She could understand why he *thought* she was brave….that one time. Maybe she was. But not any longer, this was some type of epic cosmic mistake. She turned her head, opened her mouth to set the matter straight, but he was gone.

# CHAPTER SIXTEEN

On Sunday afternoon, Maddy was the only one to hear the doorbell ring with the clamor of the televised football game and the sloshing noises of the washing machine. When it rang a second time, the dogs bounded toward the entry with jubilant barks and paws that slipped on the wood floor like speed skaters taking a corner. Maddy made it to the entry just as her aunt and uncle let themselves in.

Her exasperated call for help reached the twins and they scrambled in just as Rose lurched into George's side after a particularly exuberant greeting by Thor. The boys lunged after the darting dogs, and Rose and George escaped to the dining room.

"Tyler, you did so nicely at the game this week," Rose said as she settled in her chair and passed the green beans in his direction. Tyler hated green beans. Rose stared pointedly at the container and then at Tyler. He shook his head slowly but grudgingly put a spoonful on his plate. Rose smiled and turned to face his brother.

"It was no big deal. We beat that team last year too." Tanner answered for him.

"No, we didn't… you're thinking of the Red Devils." Tyler frowned at this twin before sliding some of his vegetables under his roll.

"We smashed the Red Devils but we beat the Predators too." Tanner tapped his fork on the table for emphasis.

George leaned over the table to be heard over the debate. "How are things at the food bank, Dave?"

"Oh, you know, this time of year we could always use a bit of help. We ask for more donations to support the community during the holiday season and Tulsa never lets us down… but that means more work."

"Be happy to help, let me know when to show up and what to do."

"Appreciate it, George, I really do. Did I tell you about the new teen shelter?"

Rose paused to listen while putting a second helping of green beans on her plate. She loved green beans.

"At the last Alliance meeting we met a newcomer, Blane Sheldon. He's opened up a teen shelter right in midtown. Says it's more like a home. He told us that not all kids even make it into the foster system, the older ones are pretty much invisible and live on the streets. I had quite an eye-opening conversation with him."

Rose looked at Dave thoughtfully. After dinner, she blocked Dave from joining the rest of the boys in front of the tv. "I may have a problem, Dave. I think I could use some help."

Dave involuntarily looked around Rose toward the den when the sound of the crowd surge reached his ears. Rose stood patiently and waited until his attention was back on her. He looked down sheepishly and then turned back into the dining room. Pulling out the chair she had just abandoned, he motioned her to the table. "What can I help with?"

Rose turned and slowly lowered herself onto the chair, holding the table for support as she went down. She grimaced with the twinge in her back but felt it release again as she leaned back. "About this shelter....I have this girl that is working for us...I think I mentioned Sloane before…"

"Sure, she's helping you with inventory and internet sales right?"

"She's been a sweetheart and very reliable. The thing is, I think she might be spending the nights at the bookshop."

"What, why?" Dave picked up a left over dinner roll absentmindedly, pulled off a piece and started chewing. His jaw stopped its motion when he heard the sportscaster's excited voice followed by his boy's groans.

"I don't know for sure Dave, but I suspect because she has no better place to go. She's been staying on at the shop after George and I leave. She says she's working on the computer and she's not there in the morning when I open, but I think she's sleeping there."

"Wow, Rose. What are you going to do?"

"Actually Dave, I was hoping you would help. Do you think you could contact that man about the teen shelter? It sounds perfect.

"Blane, I appreciate you taking my call, I know how busy you must be."

"Think nothing of it Dave, I'm sure your workday doesn't have too many gaps either. We do need to meet for lunch if we can ever get our schedules to work out."

"Absolutely, I did promise to introduce you to El Rio

Verde. Great Mexican food. Hey, I wonder if I could ask about the teen home?"

"Sure, Dave, what's on your mind?"

"My wife's aunt lives here in town and owns a bookstore. She recently discovered her new teenage worker was sleeping in the shop because she had nowhere else to go. I had mentioned the shelter at dinner and Rose was wondering....I know it's probably pointless to ask....but do you perhaps have an opening for a really sweet young lady?"

Blane leaned back in his chair, a self-satisfied smile on his lips. "Dave, I'll do my best. Now what's this girl's name?"

Blane ended the call, opened his laptop and called out to the man down the hall. "Darius, I have to make an opening at the house, we're going to have to move up a transfer date. Work out the details with Karen but I need this to happen by tomorrow." He reviewed and adjusted one column in the spreadsheet before closing the laptop again. "This is ramping up quicker than any of us predicted. I'm going to have Morghan get serious about looking for a second house so we can keep up. Put the word out that we're looking for another house mother. Someone who doesn't interfere in our little venture, of course...."

# CHAPTER SEVENTEEN

*M*addy gingerly stepped through the double doors into Allison's house. No dogs bounded up to greet her and she didn't have to navigate around dropped shoes and backpacks. Instead she was greeted with pristine silence and a jaw dropping view. Panoramic windows looked out onto a backyard that the arboretum would be jealous of. Flowers, with colors complementary to the exterior of the house and appropriate for the season, graced the curving landscaping. Maddy stood quite still for a minute, regretting asking Allison if they could study at her house instead of her own. She wondered if she could concentrate while worrying about leaving fingerprints.

"Come in, please" Allison urged her. Retreat was impossible once Allison grabbed her backpack.

"Let's work in the kitchen," she suggested as she escorted Maddy past the dining room.

*It's like a cover of a magazine*, thought Maddy, as she paused by the door and examined the enormous mahogany table. A colored glass light fixture, resembling a sea creature, appeared to writhe in the air above.

"My parents have to entertain a lot for work," Allison murmured apologetically when she caught Maddy staring into the impressive and somewhat unnerving room.

Allison pulled Maddy into a scrupulously white kitchen. The stainless steel appliances gleamed and the starkly empty countertops shone. Maddy's eyes swept over the room and she hesitated until Allison tapped her shoulder and pointed toward the small table already littered with books, stray papers and highlighters. Maddy unloaded her notebook and the girls dove into their project. It wasn't long before she forgot her initial feelings of apprehension. Their assignment was to interpret and analyze data from their morning science class. While the experiment only took thirty minutes, it was clear that it would take longer to write up their findings.

Maddy rustled through her papers looking for the right paper. "Hypothesis, procedure, safety...I know the data sheet is here somewhere."

Allison reached forward to pull her own pile of papers closer. As she advanced her hand, her sweater sleeve got stuck on the spiral wires of her notebook.

"I've got it!" Maddy proclaimed triumphantly as she pulled out a paper and waved it. Maddy's eyes widened when she saw the blue-black discolorations circling Allison's wrist. Allison tugged at the sweater sleeve, slid her arm under the table. Expressionless, she stared back at Maddy through rounded lens that glimmered with reflected light.

"Show me the data sheet," Allison repeated. Maddy blinked and passed the forgotten sheet across the table.

"This number is not fitting in the calculation, could you check it?" Allison pointed to a spot on the graph. Maddy nodded, winced as a sharp pain coursed up her neck to the back of her head. *Another one of her headaches, and it was a bad one.*

"Allison!"

Maddy's pen slipped from her hand and tumbled to the floor at the sound of the deep voice. A glance the chrome wall clock confirmed that they had been immersed in their work longer than she realized and this must be Allison's father. Maddy's first impression of him, with his crisp white shirt and perfectly styled hair, was that the house was a reflection of *him*. Allison went very still and Maddy felt the hairs lift on her arms. The throbbing of her head intensified.

"I would like a word with you, Allison." His voice had a tinge of tight exasperation but his facial expression was contained and revealed nothing. His hand snaked around Allison's wrist and he roughly pulled her to her feet. They were halfway to the door when something clicked inside of Maddy.

"That's how you got the bruises," she blurted out. Her voice faded to a whisper as she finished the accusation. *When will I learn to keep my mouth shut?* All motion stopped in the room. Maddy was afraid to take the next breath and fervently prayed that somehow Allison's father not heard her comment.

Mr. Sheldon turned slowly, releasing Allison from his grip. "Excuse me," he said softly, ominously, "what did you say?"

Maddy looked up, caught his menacing glare a moment before his face relaxed back into a more benign expression. Slowly, deliberately, he strolled back to the center of the room, placed his hands on his hips and tilted his head in mock confusion. Maddy's grip tightened on her notebook until her knuckles whitened. Her stomach rolled, churned.

It was as if all noise was *sucked* out of the room, as if all the surrounding white walls absorbed every acoustic and left the room as bereft of noise as it was of color. She opened her mouth to answer but snapped it shut again under his intense scrutiny. He nodded to himself and pressed his lips together in irritation.

"It's really not polite to point out another person's imperfections. Pull back your sweater sleeves, Allison," he demanded. Allison obediently pulled up her sleeves, demonstrating matching bruises on both wrists. "Allison tends to be on the chubby side and it is not uncommon for her sweater or jackets to be a bit tight around her wrists. I don't think you can blame me for her weight problems. She's working on it, aren't you Allison?" He smiled condescendingly, patted Allison on the shoulder and walked out of the room. "We'll talk later," he called over his shoulder.

All color drained from Allison's face, her whole body shuddered and she looked over to Maddy with an expression of pleading and fear. Maddy blinked and looked away for a fraction of a moment, feeling confused and overwhelmed, before returning her gaze to her friend. Together they listened as the sound of his shoes clicking on the hardwood floors became more distant. A thousand thoughts ricocheted in Maddy's flustered brain all at once but one thing was clear. Allison was afraid of her father.

Allison was quick to return notebooks and calculators to their appropriate backpacks and then escort Maddy to the front door. By the time Maddy made it outside, her vision was blurred from the headache and she bent over the manicured shrubs retching. The temperature had dropped and she held up her face to the wind, grateful for the chilly breeze to her overheated cheeks. She took a deep breath, drew up her shoulders, held one hand to her still queasy stomach and headed for the sidewalk.

*There is no way I'm ever going back.*

Her thoughts were as chaotic as the black birds that darted and drifted ahead of her, seemingly oblivious to the icy blasts of wind. The dread in Allison's eyes as they'd walked toward the door, the guilt of abandoning her friend and the incredible relief of knowing that each step brought her closer to her own house and further from Sheldon's. So it was understandable that she did not hear the rhythmic clopping on the sidewalk behind her.

"Are you alright, Madison?"

*Here we go again.* She stopped and swung around. She wasn't in the mood. Her head hurt and she was afraid of embarrassing herself and vomiting on the sidewalk. And there it was. The unicorn. "Why are you here now?" she questioned irritably.

"To make sure that you are safe, I sensed your fear but I don't see any threat."

"I'm okay."

And she was... Maddy put her hand to her head, looked up into the eyes of the unicorn, and realized that her headache was gone, completely gone. This was the second time one of her bad episodes had mysteriously suddenly improved.

"Pardon me, but I sense that you are not okay."

Maddy struggled with what to say. Images flittered through her mind. Mr. Sheldon's threatening bearing. Allison's unspoken pleas. A house devoid of dog hair, coffee rings, and laughter.

"I see."

Maddy's eye brows went up. "What? Are you reading my mind?"

"I don't know, Madison. I believe I only receive what you *want* me to know." he narrowed his eyes in thought.

"That's a relief. And speaking of relief... twice now, you have appeared and my headache has gone away. And my stomach feels better too." She stopped and turned when she realized that he was no longer at her side. "It's magic, right?"

Silenus stared at her, hard. His nostrils flared and his side quivered.

"What… what did I say?"

"Sentira." His whisper was raw, faint.

"I don't know what that means. Why are you looking at me like that?" Maddy took backward steps, away from the massive animal.

Silenus shook himself and spoke gently, "*That* is what makes you unique Madison. You are a *sentira*. In my times, it meant *one who feels* and it is what we called a person with a gift to perceive evil."

"Not much of a gift if you ask me." Maddy rubbed her chin and remained quiet for a moment. "So, I'm not crazy, not suffering from some form of post stress disorder?"

"Definitely not, Madison. Evil is real. And while others feel a prickling awareness of it, you experience true pain and sickness."

"And why does it go away when you are near?"

"I am your protector… it is my duty to protect you from evil," he answered vehemently.

Maddy contemplated the unicorn's statement for a moment. "Can you switch to another girl? What if you were to watch over Allison instead? I'm really worried about her."

"I will not…I cannot," his gravelly voice announced firmly. "Leaving you defenseless is unacceptable to me and even if I wanted to, my bond was forged with you and I have no control over that." Even as he said the words, Silenus wondered if it were true. After all, the unicorns in the past were only flung into the girl's world at the moment of crisis and yet here he was now.

Maddy's eyes widened and her footsteps slowed. "But what if she's in more danger than I am? What if she needs you more than I do?"

"Then we must do our best to protect her together," he said.

"But what can I do? He's a grown up! I can't do anything." Maddy hugged herself, unconsciously rubbing her arms in the same area where the man had gripped her.

"You can do more than you realize, little one."

# CHAPTER EIGHTEEN

The sun warmed Maddy's back and turned her thick pony tail to burnished copper as she rode to the shop the next morning. Her sleep had been fragmented with confusing dream-like visions of battles, unicorns and Blane Sheldon's face. She woke, still exhausted, dressed carelessly in a random sweatshirt, climbed onto the bike and headed down the street.

The cycling motion helped to get her blood pumping and by the time she arrived she was slightly more awake. She thumped on the back door while searching her jean pockets for the key. The door opened and Rose appeared, wearing emerald green jeans, a mint colored blouse and sparkly black reading glasses. Maddy looked down at her brown sweatshirt, groaned in disgust at her own laziness, and sighed when she was engulfed in a hug that smelled of sunshine and violets.

Maddy stepped inside, fought back a sliver of jealousy when Sloane smiled at her from her perch on a stool in the back room. Aunt Rose's tea shipment from the Cultured Cup had arrived and she and Sloane resumed their conversation on the merits of black versus green teas. Maddy thought green tea tasted a little like grass, but she kept that thought to herself and slipped onto a nearby stool, waited for the tea kettle to get hot again. She listened half-heartedly, letting the sounds of female laughter and the comforting blend of tea work its magic to restore some calm to her thoughts.

"What do you think of unicorns?" The question burst from her mouth without any forethought. She bit her lip, regretted her spontaneous query.

Sloane snuck an extra teaspoon of sugar in her cup, stirred and replied without looking up, "Same category as unconditional love, Santa Claus and chivalry, why do you ask?"

Rose said nothing, but stared at Maddy with canny eyes through glasses that twinkled with her every movement.

"A girl was talking about them at school. She thought they might have existed a long time ago…never mind." Maddy drew her hand to her mouth and chewed on a piece of her cuticle.

"There are more things in heaven and earth, Horatio, Than are dreamt of in your philosophy." Rose intoned gravely.

Sloane glanced at Rose with one eyebrow cocked up before returning her attention to Maddy. "Do you mean Allison, that new girl in your science class, the one that took Stuart's place?"

Maddy opened her mouth but closed it again and felt a flush steal up her chest as she considered her answer. The subject of Allison was possibly the only subject more uncomfortable than unicorns right now.

SLOANE STOPPED in the middle of straightening the last row of books and looked up at Rose. "How did you know? I didn't mess with anything. I promise."

"I know Sloane. I do trust you. But staying in the bookshop overnight is not the best place for you." Rose blew out the candle near the register and turned to walk with Sloane toward the break room. "I'd like to talk to you about another option."

"That's just it Rose, I don't have a lot of options. I don't make enough money to pay for an apartment. Not that you don't pay me well..." she rushed to add. "My mom has left town and I don't have anywhere to go." Sloane's voice hitched as she finished. "I promise nothing will happen."

"Sloane, love, I have an idea that I think you'll like. Dave found out about a teen home in our area. He has arranged for you to stay there... if you like. You can still go to school and I hope you'll still work with us here." Rose looked intently at Sloane. "You'll only stay there if you're happy with the arrangement."

"What's the catch?"

Rose looked startled and then a little sad at the suspicion in Sloane's voice. "Let's go see tomorrow. George and I will go with you in the morning to check it out."

"What about the shop? Who's going to open the shop?"

"Don't worry about the shop sweetheart, we can open a bit late. Let's get your things and you can spend the night on the sofa at our house. I can't promise it will be the most comfortable bed you've had but it will be better than the club chair." Rose winked at Sloane and pulled her purse over her shoulder while motioning Sloane to grab her things too. They walked toward the back of the shop, turning off lights as they went. Rose opened the back door and then stumbled in the darkness of the alley. Sloane grabbed her arm and they walked together toward the car.

"I'll feel so much better once I know that you're safe, Sloane."

# CHAPTER NINETEEN

"Fighting fires is serious business, George," TJ announced as he unfastened his seatbelt and climbed out of the car.

"I agree, now let's take a look inside," replied George. It took him a moment longer to pull his lanky body out of the car. He paused to lean on the door frame while his hip muscles tightened and then winced when he took the first few steps toward the fire station bay. One of the firemen noticed the car pull up and met them as they entered.

"Hello, I'm George and this is my friend TJ. We'd love to take a peek around if you don't mind." TJ was already looking upward, to the rack holding the jackets and helmets.

Carl grabbed the nearest helmet and placed it on TJ's head. TJ flipped the clear visor down and and listened to the fireman make small talk with George. His eyes kept sliding over to the side of the bay. Carl caught the direction of TJ's attention and motioned toward the red vehicle. "Would you like me to turn on the fire truck lights?"

"While fire truck is the often used generic term, I believe fire apparatus is the correct term for this fire fighting vehicle since it has been customized," TJ answered as he continued his exam of the hoses. Carl froze, his hand on the door handle. "Well, that is certainly correct, but how'd you know that?"

"I like to read," TJ answered simply.

"A lot... he reads a lot, and mostly about firefighting." George added.

"But not exclusively, I read about other subjects too..." TJ said in an apologetic voice.

"We have some guests," Carl bellowed upward into the living quarters of the station.TJ and George watched as one by one, men slid down the fire pole. The first man was a large man and he walked toward George, extending his hand out. He had a wide smiling face with a thick mustache that dropped at the sides of his mouth only to rise up again in a curl. His heavy boots made clomping noises as he traveled across the bay.

"Good afternoon sir, they call me Bear."

"Nice to meet you. Bear. I'm George and that's TJ over by the *fire apparatus*."

Bear looked toward the direction that George was pointing. TJ turned away from the brass panel that he was examining and peered through the clear visor at the massive man standing before him.

"Good afternoon, Bear. Do you know when fire hydrants were invented?"

"The fire hydrant was invented in the early 1800's," Bear replied, glancing at Carl and scratching his head.

"Correct."

A young man was the last down the pole. He pulled the side of his pants upward as he walked, the belt a useless concept against his wiry frame. Carl ended the introductions with him. TJ approached the new recruit. "Congratulations," he said seriously, "on joining a group of professional fire fighters that have been organized since 1919." The young man looked startled for a second and then bent over and shook TJ's hand.

The helmet tilted on TJ's head and he took a moment to straighten it before turning toward Bear again. "I assume your name comes from the campaign in 1944 to educate the public on forest fires?"

"Nah," replied Bear, shaking his head and tugging on his mustache. He swiveled in place, mumbled something about checking the hoses and walked across the bay.

Carl smiled at George and TJ. "He doesn't like to tell the story but I don't mind..."

"It was evening and we had just arrived at a small bungalow in mid-town. Flames were already engulfing the side of the house. We rushed inside and found an older woman, unconscious on the sofa. I pulled her out and Bear continued to sweep the rest of the house. I would have given up. The roof was about to come down and there was no sign of anybody else living there. Bear saw something out of the corner of his eye, something moving. He ran into a bedroom and peered under a bed. Probably thought it was a dog or something, with all that smoke, it would've been hard to tell. Until she started screaming anyway. Bear knew that he looked a fright with all his equipment on so he pulled off his air mask and grabbed a teddy bear she must've dropped near the bed. He waved the teddy bear in front of her, pleading with her to come out. When she reached for the bear, he grabbed her arm and then carried the little girl like a football as he charged out the door. The roof caved in behind them. Both of them had to be treated for smoke inhalation. Anyway, when the paramedics tried to separate the little tike from him, she grabbed him around the neck and screamed 'my honey bear'. He climbed in the ambulance and stayed with her until her relatives could be found."

TJ absorbed the information and went to stand beside Bear who was doing his best to ignore the group. He flipped open his visor and looked up at Bear with serious brown eyes. "Honey Bears are another name for the American Black Bear. They're strong, dexterous and have better eyesight and hearing compared to humans. Also, they're protective of their young. That must be why she called you honey bear."

# CHAPTER TWENTY

*M*addy tucked her ears underneath her cap just as the sun started its ascent over the horizon. With the exception of the periodic snoring from the floor beside the stove, the kitchen was silent. But in a short space of time the boys would be stumbling over dogs to sit at the table where they would each inhale several large bowls of cereal. The kitchen door squeaked and Thor raised his head groggily but quickly dropped it again. Maddy stumbled in the dim light outside but once she had the bike in the driveway, her movements became automatic, as if the bike's metal frame merged with her own. The wind pushed incessantly at her face, the day promised to be colder, more overcast compared to yesterday. She knew her morning rides wouldn't last much longer.

Maddy reviewed the direction of today's ride in her head. She would never let her mind wander as it did *that* day. Maddy always knew exactly where she was as she rode, and more importantly, she knew exactly where she wasn't. And while she did not know precisely what street that house was on, she had no intention of getting even close to the neighborhood where the trouble started. She still had an uncomfortable feeling about that day, despite what her dad said.

Maddy adjusted her gears; she stayed seated despite the incline and felt the slight burn in her legs as a result. Pumpkins, gourds and hay bales accented many of the midtown houses. Some homes, she saw with a smile, took the Halloween theme to another level. Phantoms were strung on zip lines ready to astound trick or treaters. Electric cords ran to red-eyed zombies and strobe lights pulsed on a trio of wire framed ghosts.

Her breath caught as she rounded the corner. *Impossible,* her mind insisted. She raised on her legs, pedaled faster, took deep breaths through a dry mouth and thickened throat.

*Impossible.*

She glanced sideways, half expecting to see the man with the leather coat pull out of the drive in his dark sedan. But the driveway was empty, and although the house was a bungalow with the same color and shape, it obviously was not the *same* house. Toys littered the porch and the paint was faded and chipped.

It's a different house, she reassured herself. She slowed, took another glimpse behind her, tried to relax her grip on the handlebars.

Maddy's head popped up at the sound of pounding hoofbeats. "Silenus, it's all okay. I got frightened but it was just my imagination." Her voice was low, raspy and breathy.

"And what frightened you, milady?"

Maddy pushed faster again, now eager to head home after her fright. The unicorn increased his tempo, easily matched her speed. "It's silly, really. I thought I saw a kidnapping once and the house over there reminded me of it all."

"I don't think I understand, what part of that is silly?"

"Well, my dad thinks I saw a family fight, not a kidnapping."

"And what do you think?"

"He's probably right, it is a little far-fetched."

"As far-fetched as a unicorn, Madison?"

Maddy didn't respond but regarded a car as it turned the corner onto their street and drove toward them. She watched the driver carefully but saw no signs that he was aware of the massive beast that trotted by her side.

"About that, Silenus, am I the only one that can see you?"

"That is almost correct. Only those to whom we are pledged can see us… And the enemy, of course."

"What enemy?"

"My duty is to protect you Madison. If you are threatened, I will engage the enemy. In those moments, the enemy will see me… it is only honorable after all."

"It must be terribly hard to kill a unicorn, right?"

"Not impossible, of course, but we do die if our heart is pierced."

Maddy chewed on her lip as she asked the next question. "Have you always been successful protecting the ladies you have been pledged to?"

"No, Madison, I have not." Silenus looked at her directly, unwavering. "And I can assure you I have wounds inside my heart that continue to pain me far beyond these inconsequential slashes on my hide."

# CHAPTER TWENTY-ONE

*S*loane's gaze followed George as he moved around the kitchen. He poured tea into an oversized brown cup and sliced the bagel to put into the toaster. "Sure you won't have one?" he asked over his shoulder.

"Maybe later," Sloane said. She twisted the paper napkin in her hand, occasionally dropping the tight coil in her lap to tuck her hair behind her ear. She was dressed, woke early to use the single bathroom before either George or Rose stirred from their warm bed. She was determined not to be a bother to anyone. The backpack and small box that sat by the front door held all of her worldly belongings. Well, except for the cosmetic bag in the drawer at work, she left that at the shop on purpose, needed some tie back to the shop.

*She looks tired,* George thought as he spread the cream cheese on the bagel and took a bite. A noise outside caught his attention and he squinted as he looked over the sink into the backyard. *Another squirrel...* Sloane was stiff, uncomfortable, and he wished Rose would come out of the bedroom and fix it.

"Is everybody ready?" Rose stepped into the kitchen,

prompting an spontaneous grin from Sloane. Rose was wearing a purple velour sweatsuit with a sparkling design on her jacket. With her red hair she looked like an exotic flower. A large, energetic orchid perhaps. "George, did you offer Sloane a bagel?" She absentmindedly wiped the crumbs he left on the countertop into the sink.

"I did, but I don't think she's hungry yet," George answered.

~

Rose glanced at Sloane. The girl was quiet, withdrawn. *Reminds me of the day she showed up at the bookstore,* Rose thought. "Never mind, let's pack up something for you to eat later. We'll go by the teen house and see how that works out and then we can drop you off at school. After school, you'll come by the shop and we can all talk about how the day went."

Rose had a plan, she always had a plan, George thought gratefully.

Sloane felt her heart slow down to a more relaxed rate and let out a breath she didn't know she was holding. It had been a long night on the sofa.

George handed Rose a travel mug and then grabbed the keys. The trio made their way to the car and then sat in the small Kia watching the windshield wipers sweep the condensation away. The car was chilly despite the heater and Sloane shivered alone in the back seat. George looked over his shoulder to back up and frowned when he saw how desolate she looked.

"Sloane, you look like you're freezing, you should wear a heavier coat, love." Sloane nodded at Rose, looked out the side window and made no further small talk on the drive. When they arrived, she was encouraged to see that the teen house looked like any other house on the street. She wasn't sure what she was expecting but *ordinary* was good. They walked up the steps together and Sloane gained confidence but still maneuvered her body behind George's when he rang the doorbell.

The door opened and the dark haired woman looked puzzled at first. Her gaze bounced off Rose and then George before finally landing on Sloane. She smiled warmly at her visitors. "You must be Sloane," she said. "Come in, I've been expecting you." She opened the door wider and the warm air rushed out in greeting. Rose leaned in, anxious to get out of the chilly weather. George followed, putting a hand on Sloane's back to guide her into the room.

The den reminded Sloane of the bookstore. The walls were a buttery yellow and a muted sage rug warmed up the aged wooden floor. A fire crackled in the small fireplace, more for ambience then heat. Sloane sunk into one of the cushy chairs and tried picturing herself in the same room, the same chair, in the days ahead. It was not nearly as scary as she thought it would be.

Karen, the woman who opened the door, scurried around the room picking up forgotten shoes and jackets, apologizing as she worked. "I just got everyone off to school and I usually spend the mornings picking up." She sat down when she was satisfied the room was in order. "You must have a million questions, I don't think I have *any* answers!" she declared cheerily. "We're all learning this together... but seriously, let me tell you about our home..."

By the end of the conversation, Rose could see that Sloane was interested. "What do you think Sloane? Do you want to try this out?"

"I could still work at the store? And drop by and see you both even if I'm not working?"

Rose's eyes teared up at the obvious anxiety in her voice.

She leaned forward and opened her mouth. "Of course," George answered before Rose could respond, "you know you're welcome anytime. I need your vote when it comes to the music selection." He winked at her and then grabbed the edge of the sofa to push himself upward. "I think we're finished here, I have to get this young lady to school."

Sloane walked out to the car and retrieved her things. She returned to the living room as George and Rose were saying their goodbyes. Karen held out her hands. "Would you like to leave your things with me? I'll put them on your bed and then introduce you to the other girls when you return later today."

George hobbled toward the car, the recent cold chill aggravated his hip. He started the engine and Rose turned in her seat to face Sloane. "I have a good feeling about this Sloane. This is going to be a turning point in your life."

# CHAPTER TWENTY-TWO

*S*oulful jazz greeted Maddy as she stepped in the shop. Obviously, it was Aunt Rose's turn to pick the music. She let her backpack slide off her shoulder and onto the floor, before pulling some papers from the file cabinet.

"The first internet order went out." George announced from the front of the shop.

"Yes, Sloane is really doing a good job," Maddy heard her aunt reply. Maddy frowned a little as she walked to the front of the shop and saw her aunt and uncle bent over the laptop. Part of her wanted to stamp her feet and say *I don't want to share!* Rose and George spoke so often of Sloane she was beginning to feel like *she* was the outsider.

Rose looked up as Maddy entered the room. "Come in dear, are you ready to get to work?"

"I already pulled the invoices, Aunt Rose."

"I believe Sloane is due soon, did you want to wait for her to help?" Rose looked over in time to catch Maddy's disappointment. "Hey, what's this about?"

"I didn't realize she was working today. I thought I was alone with you."

"Ah, Maddy love, let's go to the back and talk." She put her arm around Maddy, squeezed her gently and started walking.

"Hey, if you're having some girl time back there, I think we can change the music selection..."

Maddy was silent as she reflected on the conversation. *What would it be like to spend the night here? What if my paycheck paid for my food?* Maddy and Rose both startled at the sound of the pounding on the back door. Rose stood up. She gave Maddy another quick hug and headed toward the back door. Maddy got up, grabbed a pile of already cataloged books, and made her way toward the book shelves.

Her hand stilled as she slid a book, *Firefighting in Victorian Times*, onto the shelf. She wondered how many people had something they were hiding from the world. Allison's face appeared in her mind and she had an uncomfortable feeling about her. The kind of feeling that said she should step forward and *do* something. But what?

"It's time for dinner, Allison." Blane stood at the doorway to Allison's bedroom with a look of distaste on his face. This was the one room in the house that did not have the clean lines and modern look he preferred. His lips thinned as he looked over the floral comforter and the stuffed animals thrown haphazardly around the room. Allison hurriedly closed her laptop, came to a stand and clenched her fists as he scrutinized the room. She was careful to remove any expression from her face but edged a hand out to the small stuffed dog that had laid beside her on the bed. She stroked the soft fur between her thumb and forefinger, pausing when his attention turned back to her.

Their eyes met and Allison felt a small victory when he made no comment. Every stuffed animal, dainty knick-knack and frilly pillow was earned. Her parents set high expectations of her and with each accomplishment came a reward. *Everything has a cost, Allison.* Allison headed to the doorway, knowing it was best to distract her father from his current thoughts.

"Are you going out after dinner?" Allison crossed her fingers at her side as she followed him down the hallway.

Blane ignored her question but asked one of his own. "Are you still studying with Madison?"

"Not often." Allison looked to the ground and held her breath.

"I'm not," Blane spoke slowly, watching Allison as he spoke, "entirely sure I like her."

"She's not bad, I swear it," Allison replied too quickly.

Blane stopped in his tracks and faced her with cold, triumphant eyes. Allison felt her palms sweat but she was careful to keep her face flat, expressionless.

"I'm not sure I was clear. I don't feel that she is suitable." He finished his remark by grabbing her upper arm, as if to escort her into the dining room.

Allison winced and wondered if she would have another bruise.

Morghan looked up approvingly as the two walked in. "Have a seat, dinner is ready. Allison, you look a bit pale. Are you sure you're taking those vitamins that I got for you?"

Allison nodded as she pulled out her chair in the middle of the long table and set her attention, as was her routine, toward the picture window. Her parent's dinner conversation never included her. Dusk was fast approaching but she could still make out squirrels scampering up trees and rustling through the shrubs. A fat grey squirrel traveled toward the end of a limb and Allison paused in the middle of cutting her meat to watch the branch slowly descend under the animal's weight. A second squirrel appeared from nowhere, jumped on the same branch and both squirrels tumbled to the ground and raced up another tree. Allison stifled a giggled and then winced when the knife slipped from her hands and made a cracking sound against the plate. She removed the knife from her plate, folded her hands in her lap and cast her eyes down while she waited for her father's reaction to disturbing his meal.

*How can I be so clumsy?*

Allison chanced a peek at her father and let out a shaggy breath when she realized he was deep in conversation about some financial asset and didn't notice her slip. *Children are to be seen but not heard during dinner.*

She picked up her silverware again, concentrated on eating noiselessly. Tree limbs scattered the last of the sun's rays and threw them in speckled patterns across the room. When the light shifted, her father was cast in shadows but her mother was washed with streams of light, her blonde hair glowed, her manicured fingers sparkled, and her diamond pendant reflected prisms of color on the side wall. Allison looked down with dismay at her own hands, thickened fingers with short torn nails and inflamed cuticles from her incessant nail biting. She tucked them under the napkin in her lap between bites.

"I called the agent to let them know that we're looking for another house. Are you sure that we're ready?"

Allison looked up, curious at her mom's comment. She had no idea that her parents were planning to open another teen's house. The whole concept felt odd to her, weird and unsettling. As far as she could tell, her father did not like babies, children or teenagers. Especially teenagers. Months ago, her mother reminded her about a classmate from her previous school that ended up homeless, but Allison had no recollection of the incident. And since her mother and father's involvement in her school life was extremely limited, she wasn't even sure how her mother had made the discovery.

"I've got everything under control, Morghan. You just continue doing your fundraising and find me a house. I'll take care of the rest."

Allison saw her mom's lips tighten for a fleeting moment before relaxing again into a smile.

# CHAPTER TWENTY-THREE

*M*addy lifted up the glass beaker and peered at the clear liquid. "I think I'm seeing some bubbles, what do you think Allison?"

Allison looked up briefly from the science laboratory book she appeared to be studying intensely. "Maybe," she answered without more than a glance at the object in question.

Maddy narrowed her eyes when she realized that Allison's cheeks were flushed and her glasses looked a little foggy. "Are you okay? Are you getting sick or anything?"

Allison didn't look up a second time but replied in a lower voice, "I'm quite fine, thank you for asking." Maddy shrugged her shoulders and read the next part of the experiment. "Add 5 ml of liquid B to each beaker and record at what time you see a color change." Allison made no movement so Maddy measured out the defined amounts and carefully poured the liquid as instructed. "Now stir the third container briefly and note if this influences the timing of the color change." Maddy held up the beaker with one hand and stirred with the other while Allison's attention remained rapt on the page listing supplies for the experiment already underway.

"I think there's a color change." Delicate strands of blue coalesced as she stirred.

"Ok."

"Can you write down what time we noted the color change?"

"What?"

"The liquid in the beaker has changed color, can you write down what time it happened? Look! The other beakers are starting to change too. We need to write those times down too."

"What does it matter?"

"What?" Maddy lowered the beaker in her hand and looked over at her friend but Allison refused to meet her eyes. Maddy put the beaker in the rack, grabbed a pen from the side pocket of her backpack, glanced at the clock mounted in the front of the class room and recorded the times. Reading the next lines, she paused and looked up at Allison again but Allison remained silent.

Maddy turned back to the paper and jotted down some answers under the sections for analysis and conclusion, signed her name, and slid the paper towards Allison. Allison scribbled her name, bent over to retrieve her backpack and started haphazardly shoving books and papers inside. The class bell rang as Maddy dropped the completed sheet in the teacher's tray. Before Maddy could finish packing her own backpack, Allison slipped into the hallway.

MADDY TURNED her shoulders sideways to angle through the lunchtime crowd. The narrow corridor opened up into a larger room with high ceilings, all white with the a life size stallion's silhouette marking the front of the room. Cafeteria noises, dropped trays and clattering silverware, competed with the constant drone of conversations. Maddy changed course to avoid a puddle of spilled milk and was surprised to see Allison at the table by her side. She tapped Allison on the shoulder.

"Is something wrong with our usual table? Why are you sitting here?"

Allison swiveled in her chair with a look of resignation on her face. "I'm going to start eating lunch at this table," Allison said.

"But we've been sitting together for a while, what happened? Are you mad at me?"

Allison blinked rapidly and her eyes shimmered behind her spotless glasses.

"My parents feel that I should expand my relationships, that's all." She spun in her chair, opened up her brown lunch bag and pulled out carrot sticks and apple slices. The conversation was over.

## CHAPTER TWENTY-FOUR

*M*addy knelt down to unlock the bike lock. Once the bike was free, she maneuvered around the stream of students exiting the building until finally reaching a clear spot. Maddy pushed her foot down roughly on the pedal and the bike hurled forward. Cold air flew at her face, ran up her sleeves but she clenched her jaw and pedaled even faster.

She rode over crumbled sidewalks, twisting into the street when tree limbs or pedestrians threatened to slow her down and then wove back onto the sidewalk on roads too congested with cars.

Something happened to Allison. She was sure of it.

By unspoken agreement, all subsequent study sessions had taken place in Maddy's house.The sporadic barking, thumping basketballs, hoarse shouts from the den on game nights... nothing deterred Allison from a study session. Maddy suspected she liked it all.

~

On Allison's first visit to the O'Brien house, Maddy hooked her fingers around Thor's collar at the chime of the doorbell. Zeus, however, slipped past her, and initiated a full frontal attack. With an exuberant lunge he put his front paws on Allison's chest, issued an ear-splitting welcome bark, and slathered wet kisses on her cheeks and glasses.

Maddy took one look at the shocked girl, grabbed her hand and pushed her toward the stairs. She blocked the dogs from behind and was almost successful shielding Allison from further assault.

The thundering noise from above made both girls look up. Maddy let out a heartfelt groan, pulled Allison to the side and waited. Tanner's back slammed onto the side wall of the landing above. As he regained his balance, Tyler came from behind, threw his shoulder against Tanner's midsection and rocketed Tanner back into the same wall with a thud. Grunts and barks punctuated the remainder of the chase down the stairs.

Maddy contemplated her strategy but before she could react, Allison rushed the stairs. She darted around one of the unruly dogs, pivoted, made it to the hallway. With paws that slipped, failed to gain traction on the wooden floors, Zeus lunged in chase.

"Second door on the right!" Maddy instructed. She grasped Thor's collar as he, too, attempted to slide past her in his pursuit of the newcomer. Maddy moved swiftly, used a body block to keep the curious dogs out, entered the bedroom and surveyed her friend. As anticipated, Allison's eyes had a sheen behind her saliva-smudged lens. Maddy opened her mouth to apologize, paused when she saw Allison open hers, and waited stoically for the hysterics. This was not the first time her household had conspired against her, driven a potential friend to tears.

Allison lifted one hand up to remove her glasses, bent her

head forward and let out a snorting noise. Maddy's eyes opened wider. Allison drew a deep breath, wiped her glasses on her sweatshirt, and convulsed in giggles. "Did...I...pass?" she gasped between snickers. Maddy rubbed her head and continued to look at Allison with wide eyes.

"Did you pass what?"

"The initiation. The hazing. Whatever you want to call that!"

The spontaneous hug at the end of that first visit caused Allison to stiffen. The O'Brien's, after all, were generous with their affection. But days later, when Maddy's mom embraced Allison, she positively glowed.

*It was her dad. I bet her father told her to stay away from me,* Maddy reasoned. She slowed her bike as she drew closer to the book shop and the traffic became denser. Her mind whirled with possibilities but ultimately came to the same conclusion. There was nothing she could do. And there is nothing more frustrating in life than feeling there was something terribly wrong and you were powerless to fix it.

Rose had changed candles with the season and the scent of pumpkin vanilla wafted out in a current of warm air as Maddy opened the steel door. Rose was perched on a stool in the break room, a paperback in her hand, and orange and black reading glasses edging down her nose. Absorbed in her book, Rose didn't look up but raised her hand in a quick wave.

Maddy dropped off her back pack by the door and headed to the front of the store. "WHAT were you thinking to go to the empty warehouse by yourself?" she heard Rose exclaim while thumping her fist on the counter and rattling the teacups on the shelf above. Maddy smiled to herself and looked for the latest shipment to be unpacked.

Rose was delighted that the book shop traffic was increasing, more customers wandered in to explore the new store while they were out shopping on Cherry Street. Maddy spied a woman by the club chair that she recognized from previous purchases. The woman was leaning over to examine the books at her feet and the sprinkling of silver in her otherwise sandy hair caught the overhead lights and shimmered. She looked up as she heard Maddy enter and smiled warmly in recognition.

A pair of mothers with toddlers anchored to their side were browsing the children's section. They spent some the time examining books, some catching up on neighborhood gossip and the rest, chasing after the giggling tots. TJ was in his usual chair, a stack of fire-fighting books on the floor at his feet. Lastly, a serious appearing teenager stood peering over the mythology section, his dark framed glasses slightly askew on a narrow face.

Maddy walked over to the front corner of the shop where the sun's rays angled through the window and Sloane stood bent over with her head in a box. "Hey." Sloane did not respond but slowly rose with a several books in one hand, held so that she could read each title on the spines and compare to an order sheet she held in her opposite hand. Her hair was tied in a messy knot on top of her head but several blue strands had worked their way loose and floated around the side of her face. She set the books down at her feet and used the pen that was between her teeth to make several check marks on the paper.

"You too?"

"What?" Sloane looked up at Maddy puzzled. "Hey, I didn't hear you come in."

"Oh. For a minute I thought you were expanding your relationships too."

"Did I miss some important part of this conversation? What *are* you talking about?"

"Ah, nothing."

"Well, it doesn't look like it means nothing to you. You look like you lost your best friend."

Maddy shrugged and looked away.

Sloane touched Maddy's arm. "Tell me what happened..." Sloane listened as Maddy described Allison and their short friendship while she continued to dip into the box and retrieve more books. "I'm sorry, Maddy, but it does sound like her parents control her a lot. It seems they pick out her clothing, her food and activities and even friendships. It's weird. But it doesn't sound like there's much you can do about it."

Maddy leaned over to examine the books in Sloan's hand and made more checks on the paper but did not comment.

"I just lost a friend too," Sloane said, trying but failing to sound nonchalant.

"At school?" Maddy looked up from the paper in surprise.

"No, at home, I mean, umm, the teen home."

"What happened?"

"I'm not exactly sure. She was my roommate and we've been together ever since I moved in. She's a better student than I am, even had plans to go to college. She kept a file of scholarships and researched admission requirements. She told me that she planned on becoming a vet. And then she just disappeared."

"What do you mean... she disappeared?"

"Gone, she left and hasn't come back. The thing is, she has no family and no job so I have no idea where she could go... or how she could pay for anything. We were planning to go out for pizza on Friday to celebrate my job here and I thought she was looking forward to it." Sloane shrugged and then reached for another box and leaned over to match the address to the correct invoice. "I just don't understand some people. Another case of wanderlust I guess."

"Did you ask around?"

"Karen, the house mom, said that she'd been talking about moving on and that she just wasn't happy. I didn't get that feeling from her." Sloane stopped her sorting and stared into mid air. "And she left her makeup... she was *all* about the makeup, liked to teach the girls about eye shadow and stuff."

"So, are you worried?"

"A little bit I guess, but I have no idea what to do about it." Sloane stood up and stretched her arms upward and then noticed Rose at the counter.

"Oh, hey Rose. Everything work out with our heroine?"

"Not yet. She's being held in a small office in an abandoned warehouse while the maniac killer goes after her boyfriend."

"That sounds just terrible…."

# CHAPTER TWENTY-FIVE

*M*addy's legs slowed as she turned down the last street in Sloane's directions. There was no mistake. When Sloane described the location of the teen house, Maddy realized it was in the area that she purposely avoided. She made up one excuse after another. Until the last time. When she declined the last time she saw the smile slip from Sloane's face. Maddy stammered, offered an alternative date instead. A date which, unfortunately, worked quite well with Sloane's schedule. Maddy focused her attention on the houses along the street. While the street seemed familiar, she could not be absolutely sure until she arrived at the address that Sloane wrote down.

*This is it,* she thought, *this is the house I saw on my bike that day*. She'd re-lived that day over and over in her head, still unconvinced that it was a simple family squabble. It didn't help when Sloane reported the suspicious disappearance of her roommate. Maddy stared up at the house, feeling light-headed and hearing her heartbeat in her ears. She was still straddling her bike, it would only take a little pressure on the pedal to get her away.

*I swear I will make it up to you, Sloane….*

Maddy swallowed the yelp that rose up her throat when the front door flew open. Sloane's hair was unbound and caught in a breeze as she skipped down the steps and hurried down the sidewalk. "You came, I wasn't sure..." She pulled a strand out of her eye and then pulled her arms against her chest and shivered.

Maddy was trapped. There was no turning back. Sloan's smile turned to a grin as she lifted up Maddy's bike and carried it to the porch where she leaned it against a column. "It'll be safe here."

*Safe...Safe...Safe.* Maddy heard the words repeat in her head as Sloane hooked her arm through Maddy's and drew her through the front door. With tentative steps, she entered the house. Maddy startled when she felt a pull at her jacket sleeve but she recovered, slipped off the rest of the coat, and handed it over to Sloane to put on a hook by the door.

"Welcome to my home!" Sloane sang out.

She stretched her arms and twirled while Maddy absorbed it all. The buttery yellow walls, the side table covered with framed photos of the girls along with a single abandoned sock, the crackling fire, all quite at odds with what she imagined behind this door. Sloane playfully pushed her into the overstuffed chair and Maddy giggled in relief as she landed. She felt her shoulders relax for the first real time since *that day.* Her dad must have been right.

Sloane is doing well, Maddy thought, really well. And she seemed so happy. So surely there was a simple explanation for what I saw, she reassured herself. Maddy studied the room as Sloane sat curled up on the sofa by the fire, playing with the tassels of a throw pillow.

"There's six pictures, one of each of us." She motioned toward the table by the front door. "That was me when more of my hair was blue. The one in the silver frame is Darby, she's my roommate now. Beth is in the floral frame, I'm not sure that's her real name." Sloane got distracted as she noticed the sock. "Looks like no one's claiming this. Sometimes there's tours of the house so we try to keep everything looking nice. We haven't had a lot of people come through but Karen still complains about it when we leave things around."

Sloane gave her no time to consider the rest of the framed photographs but instead drew her to her feet to complete the tour. The first bedroom held a crowded combination of second hand furniture. "That one is mine," said Sloane pointing to the three drawer oak dresser. "I used to have the blue dresser but I switched when my first roommate left, before Darby arrived. It's the nicer and the drawers don't stick when you pull them out."

Plastic mini-blinds, crookedly pulled up, covered the single window in the room. Neither the sunlight nor the light from the single fixture in the center of the ceiling were enough penetrate the corners of the bleak room. The beds were covered with mismatched faded bedspreads and forlorn looking pillows. Teen fashion magazines peeked out from beneath the furthest bed. Maddy's eye was caught by the single teacup on the oak dresser claimed by Sloane.

"Is this…?"

"From Rose? How'd you guess?" she answered, smiling wryly while pointing to the floral motif of the dainty cup. "I keep it here so that it doesn't break. She gave it to me when I moved in."

Sloane replaced the cup carefully and turned to pull Maddy out of the room. They walked past the single bathroom and into the second bedroom. Like the first, it had two mismatched beds but only one dresser could fit in the smaller room. Clothes burst from partially closed drawers and the dresser top was littered with brushes, a curling iron, several vials of nail polish and hair clips. Photographs had been shoved in the trim of the mirror hanging above a dresser and Maddy looked with interest at the ones of the couple. "Beth's boyfriend." Sloane pointed to the pale, darkly clad teen as she rolled her eyes. "She hasn't seen him in two months. I think he left town. It's for the best—he was trouble for sure."

The third bedroom was locked, Sloane murmured something about breaking house rules and shrugged her shoulders.

"What about your new roommate?" Maddy asked as they headed toward the kitchen.

"Darby's great. She's interested in learning about cooking and likes to read so I'm going to take her by the bookstore. She's going to love Rose. Everybody loves Rose, though. I'll bring her by next week and you can meet her too. She's really settling in here and working hard in school. Do you want to see the kitchen next?"

"Where did she come from?"

"Darby?"

"Yeah, and where did the other girls come from... how did everyone get here?"

Sloane paused and brushed her hair off her shoulder. "Let's see, Darby ran away from a foster home but she won't talk about what happened. Jessica's mom died when she was a baby and one day her father didn't come home after work. She never found out what happened to him but someone broke into her house a few days later and she wasn't going to be able to pay for the rent or anything anyway, so she just left. Beth said it's none of our business when we asked her."

Maddy and Sloane found Karen sitting at the formica table making a shopping list. She absentmindedly took sips of coffee from an oversized blue mug, glanced up to the pantry and down to her list again, jotting down various items.

"Karen, do you mind if I make Maddy some hot chocolate?"

"Of course not, feel free, I think we had some cookies but I imagine they're gone by now. Anything you want to add to the list?" She said as she pointed to her paper.

"Nah, thanks anyway, Karen. Maddy, pull out a mug and I'll heat up the water."

Maddy placed the mug on the counter next to the microwave and watched Sloane open the packet of hot chocolate. She had the oddest feeling that she was being watched and when she turned and glanced at Karen, she realized the woman was scrutinizing her with a calculating look in her eyes. Maddy turned away self-consciously when the microwave chimed.

"Tell me about yourself, Maddy. Are you from around here?"

"I live a few miles away, not too far. I rode my bike here." Maddy felt uncomfortable with the woman's inspection but Sloane didn't seem to notice.

"Do you live with your parents?"

It was an odd question but Maddy responded anyway. "And my twin brothers and Thor and Zeus."

"Thor and Zeus? Are you kidding me? Those must be the dogs that you're always talking about?" Sloane interrupted excitedly. "I've always wanted a dog, did you pick their names?"

Out of the corner of her eye, Maddy saw that Karen's attention was on her list again and she was no longer inter-ested in their conversation. She followed Sloane back into the bedroom and they sat on the twin bed together. "They're both lab mixes and I had nothing to do with their names. My brothers picked them out with my dad's help. They've settled down since they were puppies, but they're still pretty hyper. I think living with the twins does that."

Sloane leaned against the headboard, extended her legs down the length of the bed and crossed her ankles. "Maybe I could have a dog someday." she said with a wistful expression on her face.

They spoke of TJ's fire truck obsession, George's worsening limp and Rose's penchant for brightly colored apparel. The afternoon passed quickly and Maddy was surprised when she realized how much time had passed. "Thank you for inviting me, Sloane. This is a nice place."

"Anytime Maddy, I'm glad you finally made it. I was starting to believe you were avoiding the place." Sloane impulsively threw her arms around Maddy and gave her a big squeeze before opening the front door so they could walk out together. The bike still leaned against the porch column and Sloane reached it before Maddy.

"I've got it, I'll take it down the steps." Sloane picked up the bike frame and together they descended the three steps that took them to the cement front walk. "Will I see you Saturday?"

"Of course. Maybe we can order a pizza and have it delivered to the shop for lunch. Or George could pick it up." Maddy curved her hand around the handle bar when a particularly cold wind pushed against her and reminded her of her coat, still hanging inside.

"Could you hold the bike for a second? I forgot my jacket, I'll just run back in and grab it real quick." Maddy skipped the middle step as she ran up to the porch and pushed open the door. Karen was leaning against one of the arm chairs with her back to the entry, talking on a cell phone. Not wanting to interrupt, Maddy tiptoed toward the rack behind the door, pulled down her coat, and then reached for the door knob again—only to pause.

"I think it's too early. People will get suspicious." Karen's voice was strident as she spoke into the phone, far different from the soft Southern drawl she demonstrated earlier.

Maddy hesitated for a moment before launching herself out the door, back outside. She shivered as she ran down the steps.

# CHAPTER TWENTY-SIX

"*I*'m glad I went to see her, Aunt Rose, it meant a lot to Sloane. She seems happy there." Maddy dusted another book and returned it to its proper spot on the shelf.

Rose stood at the front of the store and looked out the large display window with a soft smile on her face. "I'm glad you went too. I've been thinking about the teen home a lot lately. Sloane has done marvelously well there. But she's a quite remarkable girl anyway." Rose wore a hot pink velour jacket with light pink jeans. Purple cat's eyes reading glasses were resting like a tiara on the top of her head. Their rhinestones shimmered in the light streaming from the front window. Rose just leaked happiness.

They were startled from their reflections by the pounding in the back door. Maddy moved toward the back to investigate and smirked when she heard Rose mumble something about George forgetting his key again. She twisted the handle to open the door and Sloane tumbled in.

"Today's not your day to work..." Maddy paused when she realized how still Sloane was. Distracted and lost appearing.

"It's happened again."

"What happened again?"

"Darby's gone." Sloane looked at Maddy with tears in her eyes. "I was supposed to meet her after school and she didn't show up so I went back to the house thinking that she just forgot. All her stuff is gone."

Rose stepped forward, laid her hand on Sloane's shoulder. "What's going on? Come in and have a seat, sweetheart."

"My new roommate's gone. I was just getting to know her."

"What happened?"

"*I don't know*... Karen keeps saying that some girls will be drawn back to the streets. But Darby was different." Sloane hesitated and stared at a spot on the wood floor next to her feet. "At least I thought she was."

"Did she have any family, a boyfriend? Maddy already suspected the answer.

"I don't think there was anybody. But that's true for all of us. We're living at a teen home because we have no one."

Rose pursed her lips and filled the hot water kettle. "Which tea, love?

"Do you think something happened to her?" Maddy asked hesitantly as she climbed on one of the stools.

"Yeah, something happened alright. She woke up one morning and her life here was suddenly unbearable... and she thought that somewhere in another city, the future would be *so much* brighter..." Sloane replied with a hollow voice.

Rose called out over her shoulder. "You haven't heard from your mother?"

"Nothing. I checked back at the hotel a few times to see if she called or came by. I wondered if she would look for me. I imagine she was relieved to lose me." Sloane dropped her head and her hair fell forward, shielding her face.

"No, Sloane. No one could possibly be relieved to lose you. You are a very lovely girl and I'm sure that your mother will come to regret getting separated from you, if she hasn't already."

"Is it me?" Sloane whispered.

Rose came to her feet and put her hand out for Sloane's teacup. "Let me pour you some more." Turning to the countertop, she reached for the teapot while surreptitiously dabbing her eyes with her sweater sleeve.

"No, love. It's not you," she answered as she turned around and held out the now brimming cup. "Everyone is always searching for where they belong in life. Some think they need to go out there, somewhere. The rest of us plant ourselves in one place and work to create a life around us. You, love, are trying to grow some roots but you're digging in the wrong soil."

Sloane took the teacup back and drew it to her lips. Preoccupied, she continued to sip, her expression serious.

"We're not going anywhere..." Rose nodded resolutely. "And whether you know it or not, you've already got roots here with us," she added pointing to Maddy.

Sloane blinked, put her cup down too hastily and it tilted in the saucer, splashing liquid on the countertop. Rose slipped off the stool, drew the girl into a warm embrace and murmured soft reassurances into her ear.

MADDY RODE HOME SLOWLY, weaving down dark empty streets. Her mind spun with jumbled thoughts and she had that uneasy feeling again. Normally when she spent time with Rose, she felt a warmth inside, a sense of satisfaction and peace, but tonight she felt antsy and claustrophobic. And while Rose and Sloane separated with laughter and hugs, Maddy responded mechanically, her thoughts distracted. Rose looked at her quizzically but Maddy shrugged, pulled on her jacket and stepped out the back door of the shop.

THE WARMTH of the bookstore felt stifling compared to the liberating, powerful feeling of the night. Maddy was apprehensive but couldn't put her finger on what part of the conversation worried her the most. She was glad to be away from it, to be free of the tightness that was gripping her chest during the discussion. She rode faster, the wind blew her face and numbed the tips of her earlobes. The houses were indistinct outlines, the street silent except for the humming of her tires on the slick pavement.

Maddy watched her own shadow approach from behind and then slide past, lengthening into nothingness as she glided by each bleary street light. The night air was thick with moisture and water dampened her face and shimmered on her eyelashes.

*What's happening to the girls?*

*Are they really just leaving? .... It doesn't make sense.*

*First, a girl was forced into a car against her will, then several girls disappear.*

*And Karen's weird comment on the phone.*

*Something was happening. And it wasn't good.*

Maddy heard the rhythmic clopping behind her as she pulled up to her house and dismounted from the bike.

"Are you ready, Madison?"

Maddy shivered. She had the sensation of being in a roller coaster going up the hill with no idea how far you were about to drop. Oh, and there was no protective bar to grip as you plummeted. She guided the bike up the driveway and toward the garage.

*Do I have a choice?*

Maddy quietly navigated around rakes and baseball bats

and leaned the bike against the wall. Returning outside she faced Silenus.

"You do have a choice, Maddy. Everyone has a choice."

She stroked Silenus' long neck as she reflected on his answer. The heat from his body warmed her hand and she put her cold cheek against his side. "Have any of the other girls made a decision to walk away and not face the problem? Were they afraid?"

"Yes, Madison."

"So I could walk away? I could ignore this and not get involved. You'd probably disappear to find someone more worthy, I imagine."

"You could certainly walk away. And as such you would no longer require my protection. I would be charged to protect another young maiden. But you have already been designated as worthy or I would not be here with you now."

Maddy watched a jack o'lantern flickering across the street. She took a deep breath and held it a minute before speaking again.

"I don't want to do this. I'm scared. Can't you do this without me?"

"I understand, and you have a right to be scared. I wish I could spare you this but I cannot. You must choose."

"When I think of Sloane and realize that there are other girls like her and that something could be happening to them....I don't think I could live with myself if I don't at least try to figure out what is happening."

Maddy walked down the driveway, toward the street and the unicorn trailed beside her silently. Maddy stopped and faced Silenus.

"I could just investigate the situation and see if I can figure out what is going on. I don't really have to get too involved."

"Madison, I feel I must warn you. There is not usually a

middle ground. You may walk away now but any decision to investigate, as you say, means that you will be at risk."

"I had a feeling you would say that. You'll be at my side?"

"You may be assured that I will do my utmost to keep you safe."

*My utmost to keep you safe.* Uh...*that* was not too reassuring. Maddy squeezed her eyes shut tight. She wanted to disappear. Silenus should pick someone who was really brave. She *could not* do this... *would not* do this. She opened her mouth to tell him so when an image of Sloane's face popped into her head.

"Ok, I'll do it."

# CHAPTER TWENTY-SEVEN

*I* can't believe I'm doing this, she thought, as she pulled back her quilt and climbed out of the warm bed for the fourth night in a row. Her heavy jeans went on first and then she added a thermal layer to the fleece sweat shirt she'd already planned. Last night the temperature dropped to the thirties and she shivered in recollection of the long vigil, hours spent watching rare cars pass by the quiet house. A thermal hat, puffer jacket, her dad's wool scarf and leather gloves and she was dressed for the night.

Her cell phone provided the light to navigate the house. The hallway was a straight path but the creaking wooden stairs were tricky. She followed a memorized pattern, avoided the third step completely and then grinned when she reached the landing successfully.

Last night she had a small mishap. Half asleep, she'd stepped on the squeaky spot and then stumbled and bumped against the wall making a noise that woke the dogs. Thor growled and Zeus appeared at the bottom of the stairs. Maddy held her breath.

"Quiet... go to bed, Thor." Her dad's raspy voice traveled

from his bedroom. She waited motionless, halfway down the stairs, taking shallow breaths through her open mouth, until she felt safe to creep down the remaining steps.

Tonight she arrived at the kitchen without incident. She tucked the phone into her back pocket, relied on the soft glow of the nightlight the twins insisted the dogs needed to navigate the kitchen. Despite her stealth, the dogs woke, held up their noses in anticipation. They devoured the biscuits she retrieved and plodded slowly back toward their beds. Like synchronized swimmers, they spun in circles before finally settling into a comfortable position. By the time she made it to the door, she could hear their soft rumbling snores.

A burst of frigid wind threatened to pull the door from her hands and she struggled with it before slipping outside. Closing the door softly, she turned toward the street and peered into the darkness. She was grateful for the layers, her face was already numb and her eyes stung but she dug her hands deeper into her pockets and trudged down the driveway.

Maddy had to watch her step, the dull glow from the street lights was not enough to penetrate the gloom. She put her hand on Silenus to catch herself when she stumbled and then left it there as they walked down the murky street. Cars were scarce. Their random headlights blinded Maddy more than providing any illumination. She leaned against Silenus' thick frame. The combination of the heat that radiated from his body and his rhythmic hoofbeats lulled her into a sleepy trance.

"We're almost there, Madison," Silenus' gruff voice reported.

Maddy shook herself slightly and looked around. "After tonight, I'm going to have to give up. We haven't seen anything and I keep getting in trouble." Maddy had fallen asleep in class twice, actually three times, but she was only caught twice.

"Stop staying on the computer so late, you need to go to sleep earlier!" chided her math teacher. Her history teacher threatened a trip to the principal. Maddy found the motivation to keep awake, if not alert, the remainder of his class.

Even Rose was starting to notice. "Maddy, dear, are you feeling well? Are you coming down with something? We really aren't that busy, why don't you go home and catch up on your rest. You look exhausted, love. Such dark circles under your eyes." Maddy tried to reassure her dubious aunt but then gratefully headed home for a nap.

When Silenus stepped in front of her, Maddy was jolted from her thoughts. Too many cold nights were spent watching for any signs of movement to no avail. It was all a waste of time.

Or was it? From a vantage point across the street and behind a parked truck, Maddy could see two men trying to force a teenager into a car. She sucked in her breath. It was real! The single bulb of the porch light did little to permeate the darkness so she couldn't make out any of their features. Both men were dressed darkly, as she had seen the last time. The taller one stepped back, indifferent to the struggles of the girl, and pulled out a cell phone. The stockier man pitched forward as the girl bucked and attempted to pull away. She was clearly not dressed for the weather, the pale exposed skin of her shoulders and arms glowed in the feeble light.

"Oh my God!" Maddy whispered under her breath as her mind processed the scene. "I knew it!" Teenagers *were* being taken against their will...to who knows where.

Maddy skirted around Silenus and sprinted across the street.

"NO, stop!" she screamed.

"NO, MADISON!" Silenus' urgent command resonated in her head.

Her scream distracted the stocky man and he loosened his already tenuous grip on the teenager. Using this to her advantage, the girl wrenched herself away and starting running down the street, oblivious to her bare feet. The frustrated man let loose a string of profanity and started running too.

Maddy stood just feet from the taller man. She watched as he calmly placed the cell phone on the car hood and pulled a gun from his jacket. He raised it in the direction of the escaping girl.

She heard a loud pop, like a fire cracker, and her breath caught in disbelief. A short shriek echoed down the street, followed by ominous silence. The girl's arms flailed in the air when she was flung forward and her knees crumbled to the ground. Maddy stared intently, willing the girl to get up… to run again.

It was unimaginable, horrifying. Shudders passed through Maddy's body but her attention remained riveted on the street ahead. No twitches, no flutters…not a single sign that the girl was stirring. Maddy stared into the darkness until her vision clouded, she felt light-headed despite taking large gulping breaths. Anguished, she turned her attention back to the shooter.

And found that his gun was pointed at her.

"Come here," he commanded, his eyes dark and hard. He stood, tall and motionless with the exception of his gun hand which he flicked toward her as he spoke. Maddy obeyed without a thought, taking small wooden steps to cross the street.

He grinned a wicked smile as she approached and he had a chance to examine her. "What a remarkable coincidence, you'll make an adequate replacement for her." He turned, appearing bored, as he watched the return of his partner.

The shorter man halted his clumsy jog to stand in front of the shooter. A crimson flush crept up his neck as he glared at the taller man. "You could have hit me!" he complained, jutting out his chin. "I could *hear* the bullet whizzing by my ear!" He leaned forward to place his hands on his knees before shaking a pudgy finger at his partner's face. His bulbous nose flared with each breath and drops of saliva spit out of his thick lips.

The tall man paused and looked down with disdain at his partner struggling to catch his breath. "But I didn't." the taller man replied nonchalantly. "Now get into the car, both of you, we're already running late."

The tall man arrogantly motioned Maddy toward the back seat and the shorter man stepped toward her, his thick arms and sausage fingers reaching out in her direction.

Maddy's eyes widened. She took a backward step, stumbled, and then took another one. The stocky man stomped his feet in anger as he lessened the distance between them. He swung his arm out to grab her jacket sleeve but she twisted and his fist closed around empty air. Behind him, she heard his partner call out silkily, "I don't think that's wise, my dear."

Maddy heard the hoof beats before the men did. The shorter man looked up, confusion and then fear in his face. He turned his head and drew his stubby arms up to shield his face but was not fast enough. The massive unicorn vaulted over Maddy and clipped the stocky man with his hind leg as he made his descent. The hoof struck his left cheek, pivoting his head to the right. As if in slow motion, Maddy watched his head snap backwards, his feet twist underneath him, and his body topple over to collapse in an unconscious heap.

The unicorn, once landed, continued its forward assault.

The shooter, only temporarily stunned by its appearance, narrowed his eyes and coolly turned to face the animal. Widening his legs, he raised his arms and fired multiple rounds straight at the animal. Some shots went wide but others found their target on the black beast. Maddy's hands quivered at her side as she watched blood spots bloom on Silenus' chest and flank. Silenus seemed oblivious to the injuries and with his head down, he charged.

The shooter's jaw tightened and he dropped his hands when he recognized the bullets were not enough to bring the creature down. The horn was mere inches from his chest when he flung himself sideways, swinging the gun around with his right hand to crack the animal on the jaw as it passed. He stumbled forward and then caught himself, wincing with pain. He glanced at his left arm and seeing the bloody gash, dropped the useless gun and pressed his right palm tightly against the wound. His eyes darted left and right looking for shelter or another weapon.

Silenus halted his charge and turned around in place to stare at his opponent. He swished his tail once, hard.

"Run Madison!" Silenus insisted.

The unicorn rose up on his hind legs, thrashed his head and bared his teeth. His mane whipped at his neck, rose and cascaded to the opposite side. Hooves battered the earth. But his attention never wavered from the man standing before him.

Maddy *wanted* to help but she stood rooted in place. Her mouth was dry, her vision was tunneling, and her head was throbbing. She had never been so scared in her whole life. She also wanted to run, to get away as fast as she possibly could, but this was Silenus and she would not abandon him. So she stood, helplessly, and watched as the assault continued.

Silenus lowered his head and advanced toward the man.

As the unicorn picked up speed, the man flung himself onto the driveway, but it was too late. He rolled on the hard pavement, glanced to where his shredded pants revealed torn skin, whimpered in pain. He gritted his teeth, used his good arm to drag himself toward the protection of the car and left a trail of blood behind him.

Silenus vaulted across the street and positioned himself in front of Maddy when the shorter man started to rouse. The man moved slowly, used both arms to push his chest up, shook his head as if to clear it and rose up on unsteady feet. His jaw dropped when his gaze fell on her and the huge unicorn standing protectively by her side.

Silenus tossed his head and snorted with wild and angry eyes. He reared, stomped, and pebbles flew upward and scattered. The stocky man stepped backward, threw his arms up protectively but then changed his mind. He spun in place, swinging his arms and pumping his pudgy legs, he scrambled away from the beast.

A fearful backward glance almost caused him to lose his balance but he righted himself and continued his flight. Silenus charged. The man launched himself at the car, wretched the driver's door open and flung himself in the seat. Silenus veered sharply to the side as the man slammed the door shut. Seconds passed and the car came to life, the revving engine shattering the quiet night.

Silenus circled around until he once more stood in front of Maddy. She put her hand on his warm chest, leaned into his solid frame, felt his racing heart. Still nervous, she tilted her head to peer under his neck at the man in the driveway and the other who sought shelter in the car.

"No, Madison, it would be best if you did not look." Silenus took a single step forward, blocked her view of the driveway.

The driver gunned the engine and Maddy heard two loud

thuds as the tires hit an obstruction and slammed back onto the ground. An agonizing scream from the same direction was cut short and the night returned to an eerie silence.

"You must go now."

Maddy needed no further encouragement. Turning a direction opposite from where the girl still lay and the car drove off, she ran. Tears fell down her face and sobs choked her throat. She couldn't think straight, the streets, her location, were all a blur. Behind her, sensing her confusion and panic, Silenus surged forward to guide her.

Maddy was breathless, her throat burned with the cold air and her legs felt weak and wobbly. Silenus finally slowed but Maddy kept her hand anchored on his soft neck as they walked down the last murky street. He nickered when they arrived at her driveway. She turned to face him, gasped at what the bleary street lights revealed. Rivulets of blood stained his chest and shoulders.

"I will recover, Madison. Please go inside." Silenus, forever somber and dignified, returned her gaze with gentle eyes.

Maddy finally nodded and headed toward the kitchen door. Her hands felt swollen, clumsy in the cold, and she struggled a moment with the knob before the door swung open and her body tumbled forward into the warmth.

The dogs padded across the kitchen floor to greet her but her focus was on just making it to the comfort of her room. Thor blocked her path, she absentmindedly shoved this thick frame away and grabbed for the bannister.

By the time she made it to her room, her vision was shimmery, dark around the edges, and she could hear the whooshing sound of her own heart echoing in her ears. She closed the door behind her, making no attempt to convince the dogs to return to the kitchen. A few steps into the room, her legs gave out and she fell forward, her hands instinctively reaching out for the support of the bed. Her fingers missed, grazed the mattress edge and pulled the faded quilt into a pile beside her.

She laid quietly, listened as the noises of the house replaced the heartbeat in her ears. The scratching of tree limbs against the house, the squeak of someone's bed as they rolled over, the tapping noises of dog paws as Thor and Zeus paced around her, agitated and uneasy.

*Did he really kill her? Who was she?*

Maddy's mind replayed the girl's scream in her head until Maddy, herself, made a short bereft cry and rolled over into a fetal position. She dragged the quilt over her body, clutched the edges in quivering fingers. Sobbed. Each exhalation through her tight throat ended with a quiet moan, one that she attempted, unsuccessfully, to muffle with her bedspread. Zeus stood guard with his hackles raised, while Thor came forward, nuzzled her neck. Maddy felt the tickle in her hair but the vision of the girl collapsing in the street played out in her head and she lay unresponsive, paralyzed by the dreadful scene.

Thor laid his thick body at her back, rested his head on his front paws, and edged his nose toward her neck. Maddy tucked her hands underneath the quilt but the tremors traveled down her arms, spread across her body until she was shaking violently. Zeus whined anxiously, nudged her face and licked at the tears that trailed down her cheek. She extended her arm around his body, drew him closer, pushed her face into his thick fur and wept. *What have I done?....what have I done?*

# CHAPTER TWENTY-EIGHT

*M*addy woke up startled and confused. The boys were arguing again. Loudly. She opened her eyes to see Zeus' thick fur inches from her face. Using a hand to prop herself up, she saw that she was still on her bedroom floor. She had thrown the quilt off some time in the night when the combined heat of the dogs and her own winter jacket became too much. The dogs roused as she moved, glancing to check on her before climbing to their feet and bumping each other as they headed toward the closed door. Maddy opened the door, then numbly watched the dogs race down the hall and turn to descend the stairs. *Oh my God. Sloane.*

Maddy raked her hands through her hair and tried to gather her thoughts. She'd been so scared, overwhelmed and exhausted last night that she'd curled up on the floor and cried until she fell asleep. Now it all came back and she had to figure out what to do. Because she had to do something. She just had to.

Maddy pulled off her jacket to change clothes but changed her mind and slid the sleeves back on. She wouldn't have remembered to brush her hair if it weren't for the strands that fell in her eyes. With shaky hands, she yanked her hair into a pony tail again.

The smell of coffee and cinnamon spice oatmeal drifted into the room and Maddy looked up in confusion at such ordinary smells after the earth shattering night. She closed her eyes briefly, took a deep breath and concentrated on what to do next. Moments later, she picked up her backpack from the floor and headed for the door.

She shuffled softly down the hall before remembering that it wasn't important to be quiet anymore. Closing her eyes briefly at the landing, Maddy tightened her hands into fists, straightened her shoulders and walked into the kitchen.

"How ya doing, Maddy?" her dad questioned as he leaned on the counter sipping coffee.

She looked at him, flannel pajama pants and ragged college sweat shirt, strands of hair standing upright over his left ear, and all she could think about was falling into his arms. And crying like a baby.

"Tyler, don't trip Tanner when he's carrying a bowl of cereal, it'll spill all over and then who's going to clean it up?"

Maddy blinked and looked at the door. And suddenly, she knew what she needed to do.

"Forgot something at the bookshop Dad. Gotta run by there before school starts," she mumbled as she pulled open the door.

Maddy shivered as the cold breeze hit her face. Skirting around dog bowls and the neighbor's forgotten bike, she made her way to the garage. She hurriedly strapped on her mother's helmet and rolled the bike to the driveway. The winter jacket was no help against the icy wind. She clenched her jaw and rode on.

She wanted to tell her dad what had happened. She wanted him to hold her in his arms and say "Maddy-girl, everything is going to be okay" but she had snuck away in the middle of the night. And that man had killed a girl. He would have kidnapped her if it weren't for Silenus. Her parents would never believe any of it. Never. They would think she was paranoid again. But she knew she wasn't crazy, she was caught in the midst of a nightmare come to life.

Maddy didn't turn around when she heard the hoofbeats behind her. "Why didn't you save her? Is she dead?" She looked ahead, refused to look Silenus in the face.

Silenus was silent a moment. "I can't save everyone, Maddy."

Maddy took a hand off the handlebar and wiped away the tears from her eyes, unsure if they were from the cold wind or her reaction to the worse night of her life. She wondered what Silenus meant.

Did he mean *I can't save everyone because you are my only responsibility* or *I can't save everyone, including you, Maddy?*

Maddy switched gears, leaned forward and increased her speed. Silenus galloped faster, easily matching her pace. Anger, confusion and fear swamped her thoughts. Her body was on autopilot, lifting her out of her seat for bumps and flattening her body lower for tree limbs extending into the street. The trotting noise faded away as Maddy made the turn down the alley to the bookshop. She swung her foot behind her and over the bike as she braked and brought the bike to a stop. Ignoring the kickstand, she leaned the bike against the brick wall and strode over to the back door of the bookstore.

Making a fist, she pounded impatiently on the steel door while at the same time, reached into her pocket. Rose arrived at the door just as Maddy's fingers located the key. She looked down on Maddy quizzically, seeing her standing with the key raised in her hand. Maddy reached out for the door frame, her fingers whitening as she gripped it.

"We have to help her Aunt Rose, we have to help Sloane!"

Rose blinked, her eyes magnified behind her orange striped reading glasses. "What are you talking about Maddy? What's wrong?" Rose reached for Maddy's arm, pulled her into the shop and closed the door behind her. "You're freezing, let's get you warmed up."

Maddy tensed, grabbed Rose's forearms and pulled her to a stop. "Sloane's in trouble, I just know it. We have to find her." Maddy's eyes were red-rimmed and her overly pale complexion made her freckles stand out in sharp contrast. Rose pulled back and tilted her head with a look of concern.

"She's due to work this afternoon Maddy. I will certainly find out if she is ok, but you have to tell me what you're so worried about!"

Maddy bit her lip, unsure exactly what to say. "Something's going on at the shelter and I don't think Sloane is safe. Please, please trust me...." Maddy's eyes shone with desperation. "We can't wait."

Rose looked at her niece and nodded to herself. "Of course I trust you, dear. Let's call and see if we can reach her now, but then you still need to explain to me what is going on."

Maddy opened her mouth to explain but then saw Rose pick up the phone and start to dial. Images jumbled in her head and they all pointed toward the obvious.

*I failed her. It's my fault that the girl is dead.* Shame burned through her and she screwed up her face and wrapped her arms around her middle. Rose put the phone down and looked over at Maddy.

"There's no answer at the teen home. Maddy, what's wrong? Are you okay?" Rose touched her face and pulled her into her arms.

"I'm scared for her."

"I know, dear. Your uncle is due any minute. When he

gets here, we'll work on this, I promise. Now settle down on the stool over there and we'll get you warmed up."

Rose turned to the counter, stabilized her hands on the surface and closed her eyes. Her stomach was turning over and over and her chest felt tight. She woke up early this morning with a bad feeling and she just couldn't shake it and now she knew why. *Something bad had happened.* Taking a deep breath, she reached for the tea canister and, reading the label, pushed it back hurriedly. Blood Orange did not seem the right choice... *Perhaps something with lavender,* she thought.

Maddy and Rose both looked up when the back door opened and a cold breeze whipped into the small room. George whistled as he limped in, seemingly oblivious to the weather. He hadn't bothered to put a jacket over his flannel shirt and Rose shook her head when she noticed. "I saw your bike outside, Madison. How's my girl this morning and to what honor do we owe this early morning visit?"

Rose looked up and caught George's eyes. She glanced at Maddy and back at him, silently communicating her concern. George was not great at silent communication.

"Something wrong? What's going on here?"

"Maddy's worried about Sloane. She says something's going on at the shelter."

"Going on? Like what?" George stood up straighter, drew his brows together.

"Something bad...really bad. Could you give me a lift to school? I'll be late if I ride now. If I can get there early enough I can see if I can find Sloane in her first class. I need to find her right away. Before anything else happens." Maddy reached for her backpack. "Can we go now?"

George threw a glance at Rose only to be answered by a shrug and nod. "Of course, car's still warm." He grabbed the backpack off her shoulder and opened the back door.

He paused before starting the engine. "You know we're here for you...?"

"I know Uncle George."

"Is Sloane in trouble, Maddy?

"I don't know, but something's going on at the shelter and I'm scared. Will you keep trying to call the shelter and see if you can find her in case she's not at school?"

Maddy could feel her stomach twisting into knots. She was practically lying to her uncle and it felt wrong. *But the important thing was to find Sloane and get her out of there as quick as she could.*

~

"DAVE, I'm so glad I reached you." Rose slid her reading glasses to the top of her head and watched the back door close behind her niece.

"What's up, Rose? Was Maddy okay? She was acting a bit weird this morning."

"Something's going on at the teen shelter and it has Maddy quite worried. I've been meaning to speak to you about that place after overhearing Sloane's comments about it earlier."

"What'd she say?"

"Well, to be quite honest, I was eavesdropping as she was talking to Maddy a few days ago. Sloane was happy when she first moved in but she's been withdrawn again and I'm worried. At first, I thought it was all related to missing her mother, but two of her roommates have disappeared. Apparently, the house mother said the girls returned to the streets. But Sloane thinks something else is happening."

"Like what? I gotta say, I remember Blane commenting about not being able to save everyone. I don't think anyone should be too surprised if an occasional girl isn't a match for the shelter."

"I know you're right, but I have a bad feeling about this." Rose held her hand tight against her chest as she continued. "I don't know if Sloane told Maddy anything else but I agree, Maddy was not herself today. She's scared, Dave."

"Is she there now?"

"No, George took her on to school. I tried to reach Sloane at the shelter but there's no answer, she might have left for school already. Oh Dave, I don't want anything to happen to that sweet girl."

"Why don't you see if George can swing by the school and find Sloane. I'll have Emily call the admissions office, her tennis partner works there, maybe she can help us. Have him sign her out and we'll try to figure out what's going on."

# CHAPTER TWENTY-NINE

*M*addy looked out the window and watched the world continue in its normal fashion, as if nothing happened last night. Drivers sipped coffee from travel mugs, kids chatted on sidewalks on their way toward school and runners paused for traffic before crossing intersections. She swallowed roughly in an aching throat and then startled when she heard the chiming noise.

"George, I think that's your cell phone."

"What?"

"George, your cell phone is ringing. Do you want me to answer?"

"I didn't hear anything."

"Maybe we should turn down the music a little?" Maddy reached over to adjust the dial and "Every Breath You Take" faded into the background. George took one hand off the wheel and slid it into his jacket to systematically rummage through his pockets until he located the phone and handed it to Maddy.

"It was Aunt Rose. We missed her call."

George put his hand back on the wheel and leaned forward to look down a street for cross traffic. "Go ahead and call her."

"Aunt Rose, it's Maddy, George is driving. Yes, we're almost at the school. Will they let him do that? Take her out of school like that? Ok, I'll tell him. Yes, that would make me feel a lot better. You and Uncle George will stay with her? Thanks, Aunt Rose."

~

"THOMAS, it's Dave. Do you have a moment?"

"Sure, what can I help you with?"

"I think there may be something going on at the new teen shelter. Maybe just some overactive girls' imaginations."

"Oh, I don't think imagination has anything to do with it. I just got a call from a reporter. There was an homicide there last night. Two victims."

"What? Do you know anything else?"

"Nothing. But what prompted you to call in the first place? You obviously didn't know about the this...."

"Rose, that's Emily's aunt by the way, overheard my daughter talking to one of the girls who lives at the shelter. They've been worried something happened to another resident. The house mother said she ran away but Sloane didn't believe it. Like I said, I thought maybe it was just the girl's overactive imagination, but now?"

"I'd like to talk to the girl myself if that would be possible. I'm on my way back to Tulsa, is there any chance I could see her today? I need to figure out what's going on. Since the teen shelter became part of the Alliance, we have an obligation to make sure the girls are in safe environment."

"George is on his way to see if she's at school today. I'll

call and tell him to pick her up when he finds her and then swing by your office later, if that's okay."

"I'll let my receptionist know."

"And let me know what's going on... Please."

"Of course, Dave."

# CHAPTER THIRTY

*D*amage control, thought Blane. It's just a matter of a few days and this will all blow over. Blane sat at the kitchen table of the teen house, his chin in his hand, staring into mid-air. The police had been there for hours questioning both him and his staff. He picked up his coffee mug from the kitchen table to take a sip and made a sound of annoyance when he realized it was empty.

When the sun came up, he could make out the progress of the forensic team taking photographs and measurements. Daylight also brought with it the curious neighbors. He watched a man in a blue bathrobe, steaming cup in his hand, doggedly following one of the investigators. Thankfully, the bodies had been moved much earlier. He wondered what his responsibilities were with that process, maybe Morghan would know how to handle that.

Blane jumped, his thoughts scattering, when he heard knocking at the back door. Darius stood at the kitchen door and Blane nodded brusquely, waited for him to enter.

"The news crew is here, in fact, several of them are. They want to interview you. Do you want me to send them away?"

"I don't think you could, even if I wanted you too. I'll deal with this." Blane stood up and moved closer to the living room window. The street was filling with regional news trucks. Curious by-standers stood along the yellow tape the police had strung earlier. He glanced down at his shirt, straightened the creases of his sleeves and then made a small adjustment to his tie. Finishing, he looked up at Darius and received a nod of affirmation. It was *always* important to look good.

~

BLANE WALKED out the front door of the home and stood briefly on the porch looking over the scene. News reporters were already headed in his direction and he had only moments to decide what angle he was going to take with the interview, both topically and visually. Making a quick decision he strode into the street, deciding to place the teen home, with the outline of a body in the driveway, in the background of his interview.

Questions rained down on him and Blane frowned at the neighbors and news crew gathering before him. Rolling back his shoulders, he took a moment and considered the crowd, ignored the microphones being shoved at him from all sides. After a deep breath, he looked into the largest camera and spoke.

"My name is Blane Sheldon and I started this home for teenagers who have no where else to turn. This day marks a terrible, tragic time in the short history of our shelter. As many of you know, we have been more successful than I could have ever dreamed and this center has become an important addition to our community. It has literally been a life saver for the girls that live here. Girls that would other-wise be on the street and involved in drugs or worse."

Blane paused to look solemnly over the crowd.

"But, as I have said many times, we can't save everyone. And last night is a validation of that fact. I believe that one of my staff members gave up his life trying to protect one of our girls. That was his job, that is all of our jobs, to protect the young and the innocent. But last night, we failed and a girl is dead and my friend and co-worker is dead."

"I don't know what happened here and I'm not sure any of us will get the details of that vicious attack. But I know that I stand strong at my decision to support this shelter. I will not be stopped." Blane's fists tightened at his sides and he stared resolutely at the camera.

"I want you to know I will continue to be the line between good and evil." He paused again and this time the cameras would, if focusing close enough, see his eyes glisten with a trace of unshed tears. "But I could use some help. Join me. Stand up to this threat to our community and help support us in our mission."

Blane's voice cracked as he finished. He swung his body around to make eye contact with the growing horde around him, and nodded sternly in acknowledgement when the crowd erupted into cheers. His eye caught one camera and then another panning in on the body outline behind him. Satisfied, Blane held up his hand signaling his departure and turned to walk back up the sidewalk and into the teen shelter. He waited until the door closed behind him before curving his mouth up smugly.

It was a good thing he spoke with Morghan earlier that morning.

BLANE'S CELL phone woke him from a dead slumber sometime after 4 am. Annoyed, he'd swung his arm onto the bedside table and reached out to grab the phone before it roused his wife. "What?" he barked.

His eyes opened wider and he dragged himself upward as he listened to the caller. His hand reached for the bedside lamp and he clicked the light on, throwing shadows over the room. "I'm on my way," he replied and disconnected the call.

He felt Morghan stir by his side. "What's going on?" she asked sleepily.

"It's all falling apart." he answered before erupting into a string of curses.

Morghan waited him out. "Tell me what happened," she said when he settled into silence. She sat up, curved her body toward his and touched his arm lightly.

"That was Darius. He said there's trouble at the teen home." Blane ran his fingers through his hair and wondered how it all went wrong so fast.

"What trouble?" She turned on her bedside lamp and faced him again. Blane saw that the pillow had creased her cheek and he paused and watched her blink and rub her eyes as she struggled to wake up.

"There was a shooting. One of the girls was shot in the street and Byrin was found in the driveway, dead. Nobody seems to know exactly what happened yet."

"Oh, Blane! What are you going to do?"

'What do you mean...what am I going to do?" he replied angrily. He flipped the bedspread off and threw his legs on the floor. "I'm going to watch everything I've worked for fall apart." Blane strode to the bathroom and turned on the spigot. He leaned over and cupped his hands to rinse his face. Grabbing a hand towel, he patted himself dry before flinging it on the ground.

Morghan pursed her lips. "It sounds like Byrin died trying to protect the teen home and the girl, doesn't it?....Doesn't it?"

Blane stopped pacing and regarded her thoughtfully.

"It's tragic really." Morghan made a tsking noise. "You're trying to save them from the street, but sometimes their past life comes back and rears its ugly head. Why, I'd say that Byrin was a bonafide *hero*."

Blane played that story around in his head. Yes, he could work that angle. It was likely that Byrin or one of his other men was responsible for shooting the girl and forensics might even prove that. But what if he was aiming at someone else and his shot went awry as he was being attacked? It was logical, and frankly, even possible. Because Blane had *no idea* who attacked Byrin.

When Darius called he also mentioned that no one had heard from Eddie. Did Eddie and Byrin get into a fight? There is no way I would've picked Eddie as the winner in that competition, he thought ruefully.

Blane picked out a white shirt and pulled on some dark pants. Morghan came to stand beside him, another shirt in her hands.

"What?" he growled as he pulled on his socks. "I've got to get going and find out what needs to be done."

"I know dear, it's just that there is a good chance that you'll be interviewed by the police....and by news crews...." Morghan let that thought run through his head. "I know how important it is for you to present a good image."

Blane looked up, comprehension coming to his eyes. He grabbed the shirt from her hands and she leaned over and pecked him on the cheek.

"I'll get some coffee ready for you."

Morghan listened to the final hiss of the coffee maker and poured the coffee in a stainless travel mug. She stirred a few teaspoons of sugar in the coffee, grimacing at the sweetness of it. She preferred her coffee black but this was for Blane and she had other details to concentrate on.

Blane walked into the kitchen, dressed in a more somber gray button down shirt. She brushed his hair back with her fingers as she handed him the mug. "This is such terrible, tragic news, Blane. The center has been so successful and is such an important part of the community; it truly has been a life saver for those girls. This is the very reason why the center is needed, to protect those girls....to take them away from that horrible life. Remember that, Blane. It's absolutely horrible but it may bring added attention to the teen shelter. Especially if people feel the threat of a bad element..."

# CHAPTER THIRTY-ONE

*B*lane considered his time with the news crews a success. He climbed in the sports car and planned a quick trip to his office to tie up a few loose ends. Jarring heavy metal poured from the speakers when he adjusted the radio knob. He grinned and slipped on his sunglasses.

The neighborhood response had been tricky, it could have gone either way. A shooting on your street was a good reason to ask the shelter to move elsewhere but he didn't have time to start over. He couldn't be sure of course, but based on the reaction of the crowd in front of him, he was optimistic.

In rhythm with the music, he pounded the dashboard. This terrible affair might actual prove *beneficial* to his business plan. He considered expanding faster if the donations supported it. Not to be discounted was the name recognition that he just assured. He cursed briefly when he remembered that he had not confirmed the spelling of his name to the media. That was an important detail. He made mental note to have Morghan call the various news stations and handle that.

Blane opened the door to the office and looked up to see Darius. Blane smirked when he noticed that Darius was wearing his customary black button down shirt with black pants. With his solemn expression and all the dark apparel, Blane thought Darius looked like a funeral director but no one could argue that he did his job well. Walking together, Darius reminded Blane that they had an unsatisfied client on their hands. The delivery of another girl would be impossible right now. Blane absentmindedly handed his coat to Darius and headed toward the desk.

"Two packets of sugar in the latte and make sure it's nonfat."

Blane's attention was already on the laptop in front of him so he missed the slight narrowing of Darius' eyes and the tightening of his jaw. Darius turned, carefully hung the coat up, paused a moment as if making up his mind about something, but then exited the room quietly.

The client was unsympathetic to the Blane's situation. Blane gritted his teeth as he listened to the man complain on the other end of the call. He swiveled in his leather chair to better see the television and recognized his own face in the news report. He hastily turned the volume down, although he no longer paid any attention to the querulous man on the phone. This was a replay of the earlier broadcast and he critically watched his image again, satisfied with the piece.

As he hoped, the camera picked up on the emotion in his face and he considered the drama quite effective. After promising to arrange for a replacement immediately, but having no intention of doing so, Blane disconnected the call and closed his laptop.

He stood up when Darius entered the room.

"What do you mean a problem? You mean something else on top of this fiasco?" Blane walked to the door and grabbed his jacket. He pushed his arm through one sleeve while keeping his attention on Darius.

"It may be nothing."

"Spit it out Darius. I'm already running late for dinner."

"One of the girls at the teen house didn't come back after school today."

"Which girl?"

"Sloane. Sarah's roommate."

Blane stilled, turned to face Darius. "What does Karen think? Could she be just holed up somewhere upset about her roommate or is it possible she knows something?"

"Karen said she got the girls off to school pretty fast but Sloane's been asking about her roommate and she thinks she figured out it was Sarah."

"Why was Sarah picked anyway?" Blane said irritably. "Didn't we just take Sloane's last roommate?"

"Karen said it was obvious she wasn't a good fit for the home and besides, it looks less suspicious if they've only been there a short time."

"Yeah, probably. Any ideas where the Sloane could be?"

"I'll talk to Karen again and have her ask the girls if they know anything."

"Find her."

Blane opened his office door and strode down the hall. Darius leaned on the door frame and watched him depart.

Blane opened the car door, flung his laptop and phone on the seat next to him, leaned back in the seat and closed his eyes. *Maybe she's run away.* He snorted. *Wouldn't it be ironic if she really ran away? Like they'd claimed the others had?*

His cell phone rang. He put the car in reverse and raised the phone to see who he was about to ignore. Groaning, he slid back into the parking spot and turned off the radio. Taking a deep breath, he greeted the caller, "Hello, Thomas."

~

MORGHAN COULD SENSE the tension rolling off Blane as she helped him shrug out of his coat. He stood for a moment, his eyes unfocused somewhere past her.

"Dinner?" she reminded him.

"Of course."

They walked together toward the dining room where Allison was already seated. Blane absentmindedly kissed Morghan on the cheek, continued toward his own seat at the opposite end. As usual, he did not acknowledge Allison.

"...and if the weather gets as bad as they predict next week, we may have to move the fundraiser to another weekend," Morghan continued. She looked up when Blane did not respond.

Blane stared out the oversized window, his mind far from the dinner table.

"Tell us about your day, Blane."

Blane met her eyes and looked pointedly at Allison, a full briefing of the day would take place later. "It was a rough start and a rough end. To be expected really. I heard from Thomas on my way home. He wants to meet and get more information on the shelter."

"Is that good news or bad news?"

"Yesterday, I would have said that it was great news. Today, I'm not so sure."

Allison winced when her glass made a tapping noise as she replaced it on the table. During the pause in the conversation, it seemed louder. She chanced a glance to her left but her dad continued the conversation with no comment.

"One of the girls is missing. Sloane this time."

Morghan paused with the fork midway to her mouth. "What do you mean?"

"Sloane didn't return to the house after school today. I'll call Karen later and see what the story is."

"Well, that's certainly disconcerting." Morghan tilted her head, frowned.

"Maybe she's at work." Allison's voice came out as a whisper. Blane turned toward her, not bothering to hide his annoyance.

"What did you say?"

"Maybe she's still at work." Allison spoke a little louder but kept her gaze on the plate in front of her.

"Where does she work and how did you know she had a job?"

"Maddy told me." Allison froze as the words left her mouth and she realized her mistake. She continued rapidly, hoping he would miss the Maddy reference. "She works part-time at a bookstore called The Last Chapter."

"Maddy? Where have I heard that name? Wait, is that the girl that you brought home to study with? Didn't I mention that you would be better off pursuing *different* friendships?" Blane sharpened his gaze to Allison.

Allison winced at his tone and gripped her napkin in her lap. "I have made other friends. Maddy told me that a while ago."

Blane ignored her explanation. "Sloane is the girl Dave called me about, and that book shop is owned by his aunt or something," he spoke to himself.

"Maddy's aunt and uncle own the shop, I think Maddy and Sloane are friends."

Blane rubbed his chin, looked down the table towards Morghan. "Well, that *is* interesting."

Allison's hand shook as she picked up her water glass. Speaking at the dinner table was a risky proposition but it looked like the danger had passed.

# CHAPTER THIRTY-TWO

*G*eorge explained the plan to Sloane as they walked through the parking lot toward the office complex. "Let's talk to Thomas and then we can meet Rose for dinner. She'll want to know everything." His hand at her arm did little to calm her nerves.

He pulled the glass door open and guided her through.

A receptionist greeted them and then locked the door behind them. "I was just packing up for the day. Mr. Markham is expecting you."

"Sorry we're running behind, we had to pick up a few things."

"Not to worry. Mr. Markham is always here this late. If you would follow me, please?"

Sloane hesitated at the request. George put his hand on her shoulder and squeezed, then grabbed a clump of blue tipped hair and tugged. "It'll all work out Sloane, you'll see."

Thomas rose and walked around the desk as they entered into the room. He was a tall man with a commanding presence and Sloane felt her heart beat faster as he approached. *I could just leave,* she thought. *I could walk out and they couldn't do anything....*

Balanced on a pile of files was an open laptop. An assortment of papers covered the broad desk and spilled onto the floor around his chair. Thomas glanced ruefully at his mess and then led the couple to a small table by the windows that ran from the width of the room. "I try to keep this area clear of the paper invasion. You must be Sloane? Nice to see you again, George. Let's have a seat."

Sloane took a moment to look at Mr. Markham as George shook his hand. His brown hair was short with a touch of silver at the temples. Smile lines creased the sides of his light brown eyes but his expression and voice were serious.

George pulled out the leather chair for Sloane and motioned for her to take the seat. She slid into the seat warily, keeping her back straight and leaning forward as if she might need to bolt from the table at any moment. George made eye contact with Thomas and then reached over to awkwardly pat her on the shoulder. She smiled back weakly.

"Sloane, my name is Thomas Markham. Before we get started, I wanted to thank you for coming here today, I know this must be hard for you. I'm the leader of a group of organized charities here in Tulsa. My job is to oversee them, to make sure they are doing the work they claim to, to unify them with a common goal of assisting those in our community with a variety of needs. Obviously, with the news reports today regarding the two deaths near the teen center I'm concerned. I've already put in a call to Blane Sheldon, you probably know him?"

Thomas paused and waited for her to answer. She nodded her head meekly and he continued, leaning forward and moving to the edge of his seat as he spoke.

"George and Rose told me that you had concerns *before*

today. They mentioned that you've had several roommates disappear. Is that true?"

"At first, I thought my first roommate just moved on, unhappy at the home or something. That's what Karen told us. But when Darby disappeared…"

"You don't think that anymore?" He stood up, moved to the desk, rifled through the mess and returned with a blank sheet of paper and pen.

SLOANE LOOKED AROUND THE ROOM, reluctant to respond. Her eye caught several photographs on the wall behind on his desk. One picture showed Thomas Markham with his arm around the shoulder of a brown haired woman, obviously his wife. Another, a distance shot of a trio of happy skiers. Lastly, a teenage girl with wavy blonde hair and her father's smile.

Thomas caught the direction of her gaze. "That's my daughter, Sloane. She's probably around your age. So this is important to me. That girl in the street today was someone else's daughter. I can't seem to get that thought out of my head." Thomas Markham shook his head and gripped the pen harder. "And if something is happening to these girls, we need to get to the bottom of it."

Sloane looked up at George.

"I trust him Sloane. I trust him and I know Rose trusts him too."

Sloane looked at George for a moment longer before nodding to herself and turning to face Mr Markham.

"I've noticed some odd things, I not sure it'll help but…."

By the end of the story, Sloane's hands were shaking. She moved them into her lap and clasped them tighter.

"Well, I don't think it's a good idea to return there tonight." Thomas paused, glanced down at the notes he had taken and steepled his hands under his chin. "I don't think it's a good idea for you to *ever* return."

"Rose said the same thing. We stopped at the store on the way here and bought a few necessary items. She'll be spending the night with us tonight."

"That should be fine for tonight," Thomas addressed Sloane, "but tomorrow we will need to start talking about a long term plan. The shooting really worries me and I want to make sure you're safe, that all the girls are safe. The police are actively investigating this, but we should plan on going by the station tomorrow, letting them know what you just shared with us. Let me think on this tonight and we can talk more later, maybe meet for breakfast?"

"That should be fine, I don't think Rose won't mind if we open shop a bit later than usual."

Thomas escorted George and Sloane outside, stopping to lock the office door on the way. George held out his hand. "Thanks again for seeing us tonight, Thomas. I know this made for a long day for you. This whole situation has me quite worried."

"It sounds like there's good cause to be worried. Tricky though. Suspicions are one thing, proof is another….we need a complete investigation and we need to keep all the girls safe."

George nodded, wrapped his scarf around his neck as he walked to the car. Sloan felt worn out, empty, and she hugged herself, more from stress than the cold. She matched George's slow gait then slid into the seat wordlessly when he opened the door. Despite his chatter, she remained quiet, almost catatonic, all the way home.

George strolled up the walkway wearing his favorite plaid scarf over an unbuttoned winter jacket, his cheeks and hands ruddy from the cold. He met his wife's eyes and raised his hand in a wave while giving her a rueful, reassuring smile.

Rose greeted them at the door wearing a long pink cardigan over indigo jeans and a turquoise shirt. Her silver reading glasses, likely forgotten, looked twisted and knotted in her hair. Sloane read Rose's outstretched arms as an invitation and wrapped herself around the older woman. She laid her head on Rose's shoulder, closed her eyes and took a deep slow breath. She smelled the scent of the pumpkin candles burning on the hearth, the remnants of smoke from an ignored, dying fire and Rose's own special body lotion. For the first time all day she felt her shoulders relax.

"Thank you," she whispered.

# CHAPTER THIRTY-THREE

*T*homas Markham opened the oversized wooden door of the restaurant and stepped forward into the path of an elderly couple trying to exit. He looked up, embarrassed at his slip, and hastily moved backward and held the door open. He nodded to the silver-haired gentleman, who acknowledged him with a head tilt, and then patiently waited as the duo shuffled over the threshold. Thomas glanced in, more cautious this time, before entering the dimly lit restaurant and heading towards his usual table. His wife's voice startled him from his thoughts and he spun around, shook his head slightly with a grin, and returned to the table he'd just passed. Leaning down, he placed a kiss on her cheek.

"What's wrong? What happened?" Sarah asked. Her eyes examined his face as she pushed the bread basket toward him.

"Sorry I'm late. Umm, how late am I?" He grabbed a slice of warm bread and tearing it, dipped it in the oil mixture on the table.

"I've only been here fifteen minutes and caught up with

Michael. He's still taking courses at the junior college and working full time here. Said to say thanks again...he'll drop by and say hello if he gets a chance but it looks like it'll be a busy night so he's got his hands full covering all those tables." Thomas looked up to see if he could sight the waiter she was talking about but then bent down to tear off another piece of bread.

"So spill it....what's going on?" Sarah touched his hand, this time he looked up to meet her eyes.

"How do you know something's going on?"

"Perhaps the violence with which you are tearing up the bread....perhaps the twenty years that I have known you...Now, spill it, Thomas and we will deal with it together."

Thomas looked over at his wife. Sarah was tall and regal with straight brown hair that fell below her shoulders. She had high cheekbones, wore little makeup and had amber eyes that could pin her adversary to the wall. Thomas smiled at her, squeezed her hand when he saw this side of her emerge.

"Ok, we talked about the shooting at the teen center this morning. The news report implied that the employee who died was trying to protect the teenage girl. Well, I just met a young lady named Sloane and I'm not sure that's exactly what happened."

"What do you mean?"

"I want you to meet her, Sarah." Thomas ripped another piece of bread off and shoved it in his mouth hungrily. "After talking to her, it sounds like girls are disappearing pretty regularly from the center and under unusual conditions— leaving personal items behind and without notifying anyone. And Sloane believes the shelter employees are involved with the disappearances."

Sarah sat back stunned, stark concern on her face. "Who's involved Thomas? Is it some of the staff or...? You're not implying Blane is involved are you? We just went out to dinner with them not too long ago. How confident are you in what this girl told you?"

Thomas took a sip of water to clear his throat. "I believe her, Sarah. She's with George and Rose...you remember Emily's aunt and uncle that own the bookstore? Sloane works for them and ended up staying at the teen home when her mom left town. She's pretty credible, but you can see for yourself. We're going to meet with her tomorrow morning for breakfast."

"Should we call the police? Thomas, this is wrong!" Sarah's raised voice caused nearby diners to turn in their direction.

"Let's keep it quiet, love." He tilted his head toward the curious side tables before continuing in a whisper. "We're going to go by the station tomorrow but there's a problem. We don't have enough evidence. The police are investigating and I'm hoping they come up with more. Runaway girls leaving a few things behind when they disappear from the shelter—that's not evidence of anything. We're going to have to find a way to prove if what she said is true. In the meantime, we have to find a way to keep this girl safe."

Sarah scowled, "This girl and the rest of them, Thomas. We can't let anything happen to them!"

"I know, I know. But we'll start with Sloane. I want to get her out of town and away from here while we sort through this. With any luck, we can bring her back to testify..."

Sarah squeezed his hand. "Where in the world are you going to send her?"

"Well, I know a lady who is really good at raising strong women and she could use an extra set of hands when she has her hip replaced." Thomas looked over at Sarah uncertainly.

"You want to send this stranger to my *mother?*"

"Just meet her, Sarah and decide for yourself. She's

mature, once you get past the blue hair… and very forthcoming. And fragile..." Thomas' voice pleaded.

BLANE DID NOT BOTHER IDENTIFYING himself when he rang Darius. "Did you find her?" He growled at the reply. "You checked the bookstore I told you about? Did you see the other girl there? The red haired girl, Madison is her name?" Blane's lips tightened with each negative response.

"Tomorrow's Saturday, I bet they'll both be there. Find out where Madison lives, her last name is O'Brien, her father is David. Tell Hank that I'll swing by early tomorrow morning and pick him up. I want to see if we can find them before they get into the shop. We need to get this situation under control, Darius."

# CHAPTER THIRTY-FOUR

*F*our eyes reflected the street lamp as they peered into the darkness from the O'Brien bay window. A brown sedan pulled down the street, slowed to a stop in front of the house, and turned off their headlights. Thor's hackles raised and Zeus edged forward until his nose touched the window. His body turned rigid, his growl low, rumbling, and menacing.

No movement came from the car but the dogs remained restless and agitated, nonetheless. Thor quivered, shifted back and forth between his paws, and unable to restrain himself any further, erupted into wild barks.

"Settle down Thor," Maddy's father's voice demanded from upstairs. Maddy heard Thor's barks, her dad's reprimand and then a high pitched neighing sound. She fluffed her pillow and settled back to sleep.

Scant hours later, Maddy turned off her alarm and blinked at the bright light of her bedside lamp. She savored a final stretch under the warm quilt before sitting up, shivering as her bare feet hit the cold floor. The warm shower felt good but even better was remembering the phone call from Aunt Rose last night. Sloane was safe and would be staying with her aunt and uncle. The police were doing a complete investigation of the teen home. It was over.

Maddy could smell the coffee as she walked down the stairs. Her dad was in his usual position, leaning on the counter sipping from an oversized mug, wearing partially chewed sheepskin slippers. He looked up from the newspaper in his hands and grinned at her as she stepped into the room. The twins sat at the table, already uniformed for the day's game, debating the merits of their favorite professional players in between bites of cereal.

Zeus rose up and softly woofed to greet her while Thor bumped her leg until her hand reached out and scratched behind his ear. Maddy looked in the refrigerator and settled on a glass of juice and piece of toast. She leaned against the counter next her to dad, took a few sips and watched the boys devour their breakfast. Her dad shook his head as he watched Tanner pour his third bowl of cereal and then, putting down his cup, he drew Maddy into a hug. "Are you feeling better, Maddy-girl? Are you planning to come to the game with us?"

Maddy shook her head. "I'm going to the bookstore this morning, I'm headed out now." Maddy zipped up her jacket and her dad followed her to the door.

"Be careful when you ride Maddy. It's still a bit overcast out there and the cars can't see you as well." Maddy nodded and he kissed the top of her head as she opened the kitchen door.

She headed toward the garage before remembering that she left the bike at the bookstore the day before. Digging her hands deeper in her pockets and sighing at the cold, she turned to walk down the murky street. The air felt damp and misty and smelled of the coming rain. Her mind whirled. She passed by glaring street lights, walked on sidewalks shrouded in the darkness of overhanging limbs, and crossed over intersections where the stop light flashed red and green to the empty street.

There was no question that she had to talk to the police but she had to talk to Aunt Rose first. She had to know what was going to happen to Sloane. And she wanted to know if Aunt Rose or Uncle George could be with her as she talked to the police, which meant that she was going to have to tell them the whole story. Well, maybe not the unicorn part. But she was going to have to tell about witnessing the shooting. Maddy felt sick at the thought.

# CHAPTER THIRTY-FIVE

TJ swung his foot and kicked a rock down the alley. It hit the brick wall with a crack and then rebounded back. He watched, satisfied, when it came to rest a few feet ahead of him. This was his third rock this morning. His goal was to make it with just one rock from his house all the way to the bookshop. He was getting better. The next kick flung the rock far down the alley and he grinned to himself until it struck the rear tire of the parked car. It thudded and rolled underneath. He had to crouch down to even see where it landed.

"Need some help?"

TJ rose up and looked at the man standing before him. The man's lips drew up in a smile but his eyes were dark and cold. TJ flinched, tugged at the inside of his lip with his teeth. "No, thank you. It's only a rock."

"What's your name? Are you from around here?"

TJ looked around uncertainly and then back at the man. "I like fire engines," he blurted.

The man's smile dropped, he put his hands on his knees and crouched down. "I'm looking for Madison and Sloane.

They work at the bookstore, do you know them? I really need to find them."

TJ's eyes widened. He shook his head slowly and took a wary step backward.

∾

THE ALLEY WAS STILL dark in shadows as Maddy made her way toward the bookstore. An unfamiliar car was parked near the back entrance and while she could make out TJ's voice, she didn't recognize the man he was talking to. She put her hand in her pocket but pulled it out again, empty handed. No key.

The man was crouched in front of TJ but turned as she approached. TJ's face looked uneasy, wide-eyed. "Hey, maybe you can help me? I'm looking for Madison or Sloane, I'm a friend of Sloane's mom and I'm trying to find her."

"Is her mom okay? Sloane hasn't heard anything from her and she's been worried. So you know where her mom is?"

Maddy could hardly wait to tell Sloane. Maybe the two could be reunited. Maybe with some convincing, her mom could settle down in Tulsa. Sloane could keep working at the bookstore. Sloane had been so unhappy for so long. Aunt Rose would be thrilled when she heard the news.

Maddy frowned with that last thought. She couldn't hear any sound coming through the door and today was Uncle George's turn to pick the music. He liked to play the music loud, at least until customers started drifting in and Aunt Rose gave him the look.

"Yeah, Sloane's mom really wants to see her again. What did you say your name was?"

"I'm Maddy and Sloane is my friend." As the words left her mouth, Maddy could feel her stomach twist, clench, spasm. Pain, worse than she had ever experienced, shot up from her neck and lanced through her skull. She squeezed her eyes shut and clenched her teeth in pain and desperation. *Sentira*, he called me, *I can feel evil*, she remembered.

*Oh, no...no, no!*

Maddy took a deep inhalation through her nose, opened her lips and exhaled slowly. The red haze cleared a little. She clenched her hands and opened her eyes. She watched with dread as his quizzical expression shifted briefly to one of triumph before returning to an innocent smile. Maddy's body tensed but she forced another inhalation. This one caught in her throat and she struggled to keep her stomach contents down.

TJ looked up at her. His eyes were enormous in his small face and his tiny hands trembled by his side. His gaze swept back and forth between her and the stranger. She let out the breath slowly... pushing, shoving, the pain back.

"Where is she? Where is Sloane? I can't wait to get her back together with her mother."

*He's evil. He's evil*, her mind chanted. Her eyes bounced from the stranger, to TJ and then landed on the back door of the shop. Aunt Rose and Uncle George would know what to do. Putting on her best easy-going smile, she edged around the man who now placed his hand over TJ's shoulder. "She works here, let's see if Aunt Rose knows where she is." Maddy thumped on the steel door with closed eyes and a prayer on her lips.

Nothing... No footsteps... No music.

Nothing.

Maddy felt her heart sink to her stomach, she leaned her forehead against the cold steel door and took a shaky breath. Behind her, she heard the car door open and another more familiar voice. She rattled the door knob and felt a sob rising up in her throat.

Her headache, which she had successfully dialed back to a

dull roar, ramrodded into agonizing spikes of pain. Stars swam before her eyes as she turned slowly to face the second man.

Gravel crunched under his footsteps as he approached. "Hello, Madison, I believe we've met before."

Maddy felt chills go down her neck and she struggled to take another calming breath but it was no use. *Allison's dad... Allison's dad who runs the teen home.* He was taking slow steps toward her, his features emerging as he got closer. The other man stood ominously still with one hand in his coat pocket and the other on TJ's shoulder.

"I've been worried about Sloane, she didn't come back to the teen home last night. Do you know where she is?" His voice sounded deceptively mild but Maddy shivered and leaned back into the door as he continued to approach.

"No, no, I don't." Maddy looked from one man to another.

"I find that hard to believe, Madison. After all, the two of you work together. Is she due here this morning?"

"She's leaving town, she's probably gone already." Maddy could hear the squeak in her voice and prayed that they believed her.

Mr. Sheldon's lips thinned and he frowned at her. "Put them both in the car. We should be getting out of here before we attract any attention." He strolled to the car, climbed in, and closed the door behind him.

The man released his hold on TJ's shoulder and moved, instead, to roughly grasp his upper arm. TJ made a quiet, whimpering noise and looked toward Maddy with imploring eyes. Maddy didn't stop to think. She ran toward the man, and with her adrenaline fueled terror, kicked out at the backside of his leg. His knee caved in and he lurched forward, cursing violently as he stumbled. He released his hold on TJ but once he got his balance, he swung his arms toward her.

"Run, TJ!" Maddy screamed when she saw that TJ was

paralyzed with fright. He startled out of his shock, ran and then she, too, erupted into motion and darted toward the alley. Maddy felt the man's fingers brush against her jacket but that only made her twist her body to the side and run faster. She could outrun him. The sound of his pounding footsteps receded and she chanced a backward glance only to see that he had abandoned his pursuit of her in favor of easier prey. TJ had taken up precious seconds climbing up on Maddy's abandoned bike and now the man stood behind him with his hand grasping the bike seat. TJ's eyes were closed and his face was scrunched up in fear. There was no way he could get away.

Maddy took one look at the empty alley stretching in a direction that would have cars and pedestrians that would shield and protect her...*her escape*...and ran.

# CHAPTER THIRTY-SIX

*M*addy knew she gave up any chance for freedom when she whirled around, racing toward TJ and his captor. Self-defense class taught her the skills to evade and flee from the bad guy, but there were no attack and rescue strategies taught at the Y. The man shifted as she approached, anticipating her attack, but her legs had been strengthened by bike riding and when she kicked, she threw her entire body weight into the act. She aimed for the same leg, striking the kneecap this time, heard a crunching noise as she made contact. This time he didn't just stumble, he fell… hard. He cursed loudly as his body crumpled, she swiveled, leaned forward ready to take flight. Shouted at the stunned little boy to get moving and ride away. Felt the man's large hand dart out and wrap around her ankle. It was over. She was trapped.

She watched as TJ made his escape on the bike, his legs pumping up and down furiously until he disappeared around the corner. She closed her eyes in resignation when the man's hand tightened painfully, in retribution no doubt, around her leg.

Behind her, the car door reopened and Mr. Sheldon's footsteps pounded a hollow, sinister rhythm on the pavement as he approached. His dark eyes locked with hers for a moment before moving on toward his accomplice. "That's enough, Hank, you're wasting my time." Mr. Sheldon stepped to the side and motioned toward the car. "Put her in the car now," he commanded in a voice tight with exasperation.

Maddy took a chance that Hank was distracted by Mr. Sheldon. She fell to the ground, kicked out at Hank with her opposite leg and wrenched her ankle free when he loosened his grip.

It worked.

But when she came to her feet again, she found her escape blocked by both the car and the two men. Hank jumped to his feet, limped awkwardly toward her, livid with pain and embarrassment. Mr. Sheldon stood ominously still with hands deep in his coat pockets and his eyes narrowed, peevish. Unable to make it to the alley, Maddy ran toward the rear entrance of the bookshop, pounded her balled up fists on the steel door and screamed for her help.

She stole a glance over her shoulder, whimpered when she saw Hank within arm's reach. The pain in her head was making her dizzy and she held her hands to her temples and gritted her teeth until she was afraid they would crack. Her stomach was on fire, rolling, churning. Her breaths came out as moans, tears streamed down her face.

"Really, Madison, such drama. Just get in the car and let's not make such a scene." Mr. Shelton chided.

Maddy's shoulders slumped. Her limbs grew heavy, weak and her fingertips tingled. *It's over.*

She knew that if she got into that car she would never be seen again. She closed her eyes and took an unsteady breath, filled her lungs with the cold stale air. Seconds passed and one of the men behind her impatiently cleared his throat.

Maddy lifted her head, crossed her arms in front of her chest and turned around to face the men.

"That's better," Blane said smirking. "Now get into the car!"

Maddy took one plodding step and then another. And then she heard a beautiful, wonderfully familiar, noise. And like a vice suddenly releasing its tension, her headache completely disappeared. The nausea was gone. She stopped in her tracks and used a sleeve to wipe the tears from her cheeks and the smiled. Blane and Hank raised their eyebrows as they caught the rumble of approaching thunder. Hank looked upward and shrugged. The noise grew louder. Blane took a few steps away from Maddy, pivoted to look down the alley with Hank close behind. Both men reached inside of their jacket pockets, retrieved guns and raised them in unison toward the direction of the noise. Their eyes widened at the sight before them.

Three unicorns thundered down the alley. The center one was massive and as dark as midnight with the exception of a lone golden horn extending from his forehead. His ears were flattened back and as they watched, the animal lowered his head until his horn was pointed directly at them. To its left was another immense animal, this one mahogany with a bronze colored horn. His tail was swishing violently as it ran down the alley. The third unicorn was the smallest and the most vocal. It squealed as it shook its dabbled grey head to and fro. Following the example of the other two unicorns, it lowered its head to point its silvery horn.

Maddy's heart felt like it would burst through her chest when she saw the trio charging down the alley. She watched the unicorns, shoulder to shoulder, advance on the two men. The men had raised their weapons, cocky in their belief they could kill the beasts. Bullets rained down on the animals and Maddy squeezed her eyes shut when she saw the blood blossom and ooze from chests, legs and shoulders. Oblivious to the gunfire, the unicorns continued their charge.

~

BLANE AND HANK stood side by side, firing rapidly at the animals, the noise blunted and insignificant compared to the thunder of hoofbeats drawing closer.

Hank was the first to realize that despite several direct hits, the bullets had no impact. The brown unicorn was galloping toward him and its menacing horn was pointed directly at his chest, so he stepped sideways and used the gun to pummel the animal's jaw. Dust rose from the gravel when the unicorn came to an abrupt stop, pivoted, found and held Hank's gaze with dark, flashing eyes. His wickedly sharp horn sliced the air and Hank dropped the useless gun and flung up his hand to protect his face. Hank peeked through his fingers, dropped his hands when he saw the unicorn rotate its body. He backpedaled but was not fast enough.

The massive hind leg contracted and then kicked out, striking him in the center of the chest. He was airborne—landed on his back on the hard pavement. Frantically, he crab walked backward on the asphalt.

The smaller unicorn now lunged, withdrew, and lunged again. Hank rolled right, narrowly missed the sharp horn that crashed into the ground. He rolled right again and felt the brick wall on his side. With fingernails digging into mortar he pulled himself up and pushed off the wall to dart between the brown and the grey beasts.

Hank eyed the car and ran toward it but felt a blow to his back as he drew closer. Pain exploded from his left side and he stumbled and crashed against the vehicle. His left hand sought out the handle while his right hand pressed protectively on his bloody gash on his flank. With panic stricken eyes, he looked over his shoulder to find the brown and the grey unicorns both slowly advancing, horns down.

Blane continued firing, taking side steps to avoid the charging beast at the last minute. Silenus' shoulder connected with his and he spun in place and slammed his fisted pistol into the animal's flank in frustration as he galloped past. Silenus kicked out with his hind leg but Blane threw himself laterally and missed the blow. He cursed as he landed on the hard pavement.

Silenus was merciless in his attack, savagely thrusting his horn and delivering cruel kicks from his hind legs. He pivoted, charged, pivoted and charged again. On one assault, his spiral horn made contact with and tore through the back of Blane's left shoulder. Blane's right arm was flung backward and bullets spit from his gun in rapid succession until the gun fell, clattering and sliding on the pavement until coming to a stop under the dumpster. He dropped to one knee, took deep, heaving breaths and gritted his teeth as he stared at his bloody mangled shoulder.

Just as Hank flung his body inside the car, the two unicorns crashed into the metal door panel, crushing his left leg underneath. The unicorns pulled back, the brown shredded the air with his raised forelegs while steam rolled out of his nostrils. The grey poised for another attack. Hank howled and pulled his now useless leg into the car. He wrestled the gears into reverse and, with his good foot, pressed savagely on the pedal.

The unicorns lined up and lowered their head for another assault. As one, they lunged forward. With shaking hands, Hank roughly pulled the gear into the forward position and stomped on the gas pedal. The car jolted as one after another unicorn made contact with the rear of the car. Hank lost no time looking, instead steering down the narrow alley toward the street. The unicorns gave chase, but the car turned the corner and disappeared from sight.

The grey reared up, whinnied his displeasure.

Maddy let out a shaky breath. *Everything's going to be okay.* Hoofbeats echoed in the empty alley as the two unicorns made their way back. Silenus stood, unruffled and reserved, over Mr. Sheldon's kneeling figure. *It was over.*

If Maddy had looked away, she would have missed it. Mr. Sheldon suddenly yanked up his trouser leg and reached for something at his ankle. He lurched to his feet defiantly with his hand wrapped around a blade. Silenus reared up, nostrils flaring and emitting puffs of vapor, forelegs kicking savagely. Mr. Sheldon grimaced in pain but instead of retreating, he tightened his jaw and took a step forward, directly under Silenus. He raised the blade upward.

*Unless pierced in the heart,* Maddy remembered. *He said he could die if pierced in the heart.*

Maddy flew toward the man nearly twice her size, ignoring the pinch in her side as she ran. The blade was making an arc upward, getting closer to Silenus' chest. Frantic whinnies and pounding hoofbeats reverberated off the brick walls behind her.

*Too far! The other unicorns were too far away!*

*NO, Madison!* Silenus' insistent voice roared inside her head but she ignored it and launched herself upward, wrapping herself around Blane's raised arm. She tugged, used all her body weight, and finally forced the blade down. Silenus stumbled backward, avoided crushing the pair locked together beneath him. Mr. Sheldon spun behind Maddy, locked his right arm around her chest, switched the blade to his injured arm and raised it toward her neck.

"I may be wounded, Madison, but it won't take much strength to push this knife through your lovely neck." he growled into her ear. "Now, make him back off."

Maddy looked toward Silenus with desperate eyes. She whimpered when Silenus retreated a few steps backward and lowered his horn. Suddenly Mr. Sheldon hissed and jerked Maddy's body wildly. She twisted, partially freeing herself and saw that the brown unicorn had speared into Mr. Sheldon's already damaged shoulder.

Maddy pushed the knife away from her neck and easily twisted out of his grip when the second unicorn's horn drove into his thigh. Mr. Sheldon ignored her retreat to the alcove, switched the blade back to his good arm and turned to face the two attackers. He stood with legs braced, his good hand raised and fisted around the knife, preparing himself for the next attack.

Instead of charging, the black and grey unicorns came to a regal standstill, simultaneously raising their horns and stepping backwards.

Mr. Sheldon swiveled in confusion—and then screamed in pain when Silenus' horn stabbed him through the chest, impaling him. Mr. Sheldon looked in disbelief at the bloody horn penetrating his body and then sagged forward and closed his eyes in defeat. Silenus raised the human upward and flung him carelessly against the brick wall.

Blane Sheldon's body thudded to the ground, motionless.

# CHAPTER THIRTY-SEVEN

*T*J threw Maddy's bike down and ran into the fire station. "Help me!" he screamed.

Bear startled and dropped the pen he was using onto a pile of messy papers. He glanced out the office window as he stood up, but saw nothing. Confused, he stepped out of the office, his eyes sweeping the bay until finally landing on the small boy waving his arms frantically. His eyes widened in confusion and then recognition.

"TJ, is that you?" Bear questioned as he he took a few jogging steps toward the young boy still yelling upward toward the fireman's sliding pole. He bent on one knee and touched TJ's arm.

TJ turned around at the sound of Bear's voice, anxiety etched on his face. "She is going to die!" Tears coursed down his cheeks and he reached out to grab Bear's arm and tug him toward the truck. "We have to help her!"

Bear captured TJ's arm, his smile gone and his eyes intense.

"Who, TJ, *who* is going to die?"

"You need to come with me now!" TJ insisted. TJ's face was flushed and his hands shook as he tugged Bear's sleeve.

Bear looked up the pole and shouted, "Gear up guys, TJ needs us".

"Ok TJ, we're going to help but you have to tell me who are talking about?"

Men flew down the pole and grabbed their gear. TJ waved his arms, pled with them to hurry.

"It's Maddy! She's my friend. They're going to hurt her..."

"Where TJ? Tell me where?"

"She's behind the bookstore...George's bookstore. You remember where?"

"Yeah, on Cherry Street. Ok, TJ, we'll go check it out. Stay here... or go home. I'll try to figure out what is going on."

TJ looked up at the men scrambling to get on the truck. He stuck out his chin and glared at the huge man, his cheeks still damp with tears. "I'm going with you."

Bear shook his head and climbed in the truck slamming the door behind him. Carl glanced at Bear. "Sirens?"

"Why don't we first just check it first." Carl responded.

Bear turned his head to peer in the rear view window as the truck pulled out. TJ was no longer in the driveway, nor was the bike.

# CHAPTER THIRTY-EIGHT

*S*ilenus swung around and returned his attention to Maddy. The mahogany and the grey took their places on either side of him.

Maddy took a deep breath and smiled weakly at the line of unicorns in front of her.

"Madison, I have failed you."

"Silenus, no, I'm fine. You saved me." Maddy looked at the bloody threesome standing in front of her. Her side hurt more now and she pulled her right hand up to press against it. She winced as her hand made contact with her belly and she glanced down in confusion to see her fingers stain red as the blood oozed from her wound.

Searing pain spread across her belly and she caught her breath. Her vision darkened on the edges, advancing to where it shimmered in the center. She tightened her hand against her side and the pain elevated another notch. Maddy looked up at Silenus, her tears collecting and then trailing down her cheeks.

He met her gaze and held it.

Maddy's back crashed into the steel door behind her when her legs gave out.

Silenus' soft brown eyes were like beacons and she locked onto his gaze with the desperation of a swimmer going under for the last time.

*Save me.*

Maddy slid downward in slow motion, her legs drawing closer to her belly. The descent put more pressure on the wound and her abdominal muscles cramped in violent response. She moaned and dropped her head, closing her eyes against the pain.

The whinny startled her and Maddy looked up, squinting her eyes to focus on the unicorn in front of her. *He was a magnificent animal...* Silenus' hooves stomped the ground viciously. When they gave up battering the earth, they moved upward as if to punish the wind that dared drift through the alley. His coat glistened with sweat and blood, scars showing up in contrast to otherwise perfect blackness. Maddy watched his eyes roll backward and listened as an unearthly noise erupted from his mouth. Looking higher, Maddy could make out the spiraling horn was no longer golden but crimson. Matted and dulled with blood, the horn assaulted the sky.

Maddy met his eye and Silenus quieted again, returning to stand silently before her.

Maddy's willed herself to continue to look at Silenus but her eyes refused to obey and eventually fluttered and closed. Her thoughts grew foggy and her hand, previously clutching her wound, fell away.

# CHAPTER THIRTY-NINE

*C*arl and Bear looked at the bookshop as they turned the corner. Everything appeared quiet, the interior still dark. "Behind the shop, TJ said behind the shop," Bear reminded Carl. Carl twisted the steering wheel sharply and swung the truck around the strip center and then down the alley. Slowing now, Carl and Bear both looked on either side of the narrow alley for any signs of activity. A car blocked their progress and they stopped to investigate.

"I see two down...call it in." said Carl, as he opened the driver door. His eyes scanned the scene and he jogged over to the first victim. The man laid slumped against the brick wall. His blonde hair was askew, slanted over the crushed cheekbone. The skin around his eye was scraped and torn.

Blood splatters dotted the rest of his face and more blood, a lot more, had collected on his chest around a deep wound. Torn fabric, saturated with blood, laid in shreds around the injury. Carl glanced at the amount of blood that had formed in a pool underneath the man and grimaced when he saw no signs of active bleeding. Leaning in, he listened for any breath sounds. Carl shoved his fingers under the man's chin and felt for a pulse in his neck, pushed deeper. Nothing.

Realizing there was no longer anything that could be done to help the man, he stood and turned toward the next victim. The girl was in an awkward crouch against the steel door. Her forehead rested on her flexed knees and her auburn hair fell to the sides and screened her face. This must be the girl TJ was so worried about.

"Are you ok?"

Silence.

He could already see a trail of blood from the girl's side flowing down to stain the cement. He reached under the mass of hair, followed the girl's jaw line to arrive at her neck and thought he felt a faint tapping on his finger. A small movement of her chest confirmed his impression. *Thank God.*

Carl looked over his shoulder, nodded in answer to Bear's unasked question. She was alive. He gingerly put his hand behind the girl's neck to check for injuries and finding none, repositioned her into a lying position. The girl's breaths came easier now but her face remained ashen gray. Seeing blood saturating the sweatshirt, he pulled upward at the hem to see the skin underneath. Dried blood anchored the sweat shirt and as he tugged and the shirt released, the circular wound bled faster.

Carl frowned at how fast she was bleeding, at the puddle of blood expanding underneath her. His hand moved instinctively back to her neck to check her pulse. *Was her heart rate slowing?* Carl felt his own heart beat hiccup when he saw how lifeless the young girl already looked. Bear returned from the truck, kneeled on the opposite side of the girl, and opened the first aid kit. He tore through packages of gaze and slapped them over the gushing injury. It was clear the gauze was not going to be enough, the blood flow was steadily saturating the bandages. Carl dug deeper into her neck when he lost the tapping on his finger, the heart rate was feeble, thready. Carl looked up and met Bear's eyes and saw his partner's apprehension mirrored in his.

*God, she's so young. Too young... don't die.*

Carl released a pent up breath when he heard the wail of emergency sirens bouncing through the alley, the cacophony both deafening and comforting. Lights pulsed behind them and he turned his head to watch an ambulance pull up, followed by more emergency vehicles. Wary-eyed policemen with hands resting on weapons at their hips, climbed out of cruisers and fanned out around them. At last, the doors of the ambulance flew open, a pair of paramedics jumped to the ground and strode in their direction.

# CHAPTER FORTY

*T*J climbed back on the bike the moment he realized that he would not be allowed in the fire truck. Maddy's bike was too big for him, so he stood as he pumped the pedals, the motion causing his little body to bob up and down as he rode down the sidewalk. His thighs already ached from the ride to the fire station but he ignored the pain and focused on returning to the alley behind the bookshop. Horrible possibilities churned through his head and it was fortunate that a car horn startled him and saved him from rushing through a busy intersection. He waited impatiently, his face drawn and sweaty, his breath short and choppy, and launched himself forward again when the signal finally changed. With whitened knuckles, he leaned forward over the handlebars.

*Please help her, please help her... Don't let them hurt Maddy....*

THE PARAMEDICS WORKED EFFICIENTLY, bringing supplies from the ambulance to the alley where they knelt to work beside the girl. An oxygen mask was slipped over the girl's head and the man adjusted the flow from the tank. Another paramedic pulled up the sleeve of the sweat shirt to tie a tourniquet. Swabbing quickly with alcohol, he jabbed the needle into the skin to start the IV. He repositioned the needle several times but still failed to find the vein. Without it, she would die.

~

TJ TURNED the corner of the alley and saw the lights flashing. He rode further down, past the fire truck and ambulance, and arrived at the back entrance of the bookshop.

He paused at the dumpster to climb off the bike, leaning it once more against the brick wall. Brushing the hair and sweat out of his eyes, TJ strained to see Maddy through the crowd. He caught glimpses of both Carl and Bear and he wanted someone to tell him that she was going to be alright. TJ watched one paramedic rise to walk hurriedly toward the ambulance with a tight worried expression. TJ's breath caught and he felt his heart thud painfully in this throat as he watched the scene. *This was bad...worse than bad.*

TJ's attention was drawn away from the commotion by a glimmer of light slanting down and striking something metallic. He wove behind the vehicles, peered down the opposite side of the alley and widened his eyes in astonishment. He recognized the animals, of course. They were creatures of fairy tales and myths and they were right there, behind Rose's bookstore.

The black unicorn made him nervous. It rose up on its hind legs and thrashed its head violently, his golden horn crimson with dried blood. The smaller of the unicorns eyed the agitated black while the brown unicorn turned to meet TJ's eye. The massive animal examined TJ with its steely gaze and then tipped its head in acknowledgement. TJ should have been afraid, the black animal in particular, looked murderously angry. But for reasons TJ could not have explained, TJ felt no threat from the terrifying beasts.

∼

BEAR WATCHED with relief as the needle finally slid obediently into the vein. The paramedic squeezed the bag of fluids and nodded in satisfaction as he taped the plastic tubing to her arm. Moments later, they gently lifted the girl onto a stretcher and wheeled her toward the open doors of the ambulance. He watched as the remainder of the crew loaded into the ambulance and slammed the doors behind them. He took a deep breath through his nose and released it in a heavy sigh and heard... a tiny hiccup. Startled, he spun around and saw TJ, his eyes glistening with tears, hiccuping as he held back sobs.

*Oh my God,* he thought, *he saw this.*

Bear walked toward him slowly, keeping eye contact and murmuring reassurances. "It's going to be alright, everything is going to be okay...." He paused for a moment thinking he saw something large move behind the small boy but it was clear the alley was empty. Gravel bit into his knees when Bear kneeled down in front of the little boy. He reached out to pat TJ but caught sight of his own hands, stained with dried blood, and withdrew them behind his back to avoid frightening the young boy.

"Did she die?" TJ sniffed as he gazed at Bear through wet eyelashes.

"No, the ambulance got here in time. You did a good job, TJ. You saved her. Everything's going to be ok." Bear squeezed his fists behind his back and silently prayed he wasn't lying.

"She *looked* dead. Are you sure?"

"She lost a lot of blood and she did look dead but she wasn't, I promise."

TJ examined his face and slowly nodded in response.

TJ TURNED, shuffling slowly down the alley. Bear blinked and rubbed his eyes when he thought he saw another shimmer of movement, this time, right beside TJ. Shaking his head, he decided it must have been a result of the stirred up dust and the slant of the sun.

# CHAPTER FORTY-ONE

*G*eorge pulled the car to a stop in front of the red colonial house. "Are you sure that's the right one?" Rose squinted and tried to read the house numbers by the door. Sloane unlatched her seatbelt and leaned forward between the seats.

"That's the one." George turned off the car. "Dave took me here once for a meeting. Let's get going, they're expecting us." Boxwoods lined the front of the house, purple and red pansies clumped around the front entry and twin porch lights glowed in welcome. Rose was still admiring the landscaping when the door opened in front of them.

"Come on in and I'm sorry for the last minute change. I appreciate you driving out to the house instead of meeting in midtown. I really didn't want Sloane out in public until we get this all settled. Sarah's in the kitchen making coffee and I picked up some bagels, I hope that's okay with everyone." Thomas held out his arm and ushered the trio in.

"That'll be just fine," Rose answered. Thomas turned to lead the way into the kitchen and Rose took this as opportunity to crane her neck to see the rooms along the way. The darkened dining room was on the right, with a traditional crystal chandelier hanging over what Rose assumed to be a French antique table and chairs. The brightly lit home office on the left caught her eye. Rose trailed behind, looking with some envy at the marble fireplace and adjacent leather chairs. Thomas' desk, she noted, had paper piles strewn over the top and it was obvious their arrival had interrupted whatever he was working on. The oversized windows to the front yard explained how he knew they had arrived.

"It's really up to you, Sloane." Thomas explained after they sat down and reviewed the situation. "I think if you stay with Sarah's mother you could help her out, and be away from here, until we figure this out. It sounds like a perfect solution for everyone."

George nodded in agreement, took another sip and looked up when Rose nudged his arm. "Your phone, it's ringing…" He pulled it from his pocket and held it to his ear.

"George, is that you? This is Carl from the fire station."

"Yes, this is George, I remember you, Carl." George left Rose and Sloane sitting at the table with the Markhams and wandered down the hall, puzzled by the call.

"I called the bookshop and the phone calls must be forwarded to you. Anyway, I was hoping you could help me."

"Sure, what I can do for you?" George stood in the hallway admiring an oil painting. The colors were so vivid that he had to hold his hand back from touching a dew drop on the painted leaf.

"Your little friend, TJ, he said his friend's name is Maddy. I need to get in touch with her parents."

George's hand dropped away from the painting and he turned to look down the hallway, his throat thick and dry. He watched Rose lean over and playfully tug at a lock of Sloane's hair.

"George? Are you still there?"

"That's my niece, Carl. Can you tell me what happened?" he whispered in a lower voice now.

"She's been injured and I'm afraid it's serious. Can you tell me how to contact her parents?"

"I'll take care of contacting her parents. Where is she? Where have you taken her?"

# CHAPTER FORTY-TWO

*D*ave O'Brien sat next to his wife in the row of olive green waiting room chairs. He leaned forward with his elbows on his knees, his hands clasped in front of him and his eyes focused on a crack in the scrubbed linoleum floor. He looked up when he saw two sets of tattered sneakers shuffle in front of him.

Tanner wore a mutinous expression on his face and had his hands at his hips while Tyler pointed his chin and his finger toward the hospital door. "You need to go in there, you need to be with Maddy."

"Tyler, it's marked hospital personnel for a reason."

Tanner threw his arms up in vexation. "It's not like you're a visitor, you're her dad. And she *needs* you. She's alone in there. You have to go in dad, please!" Tanner blinked quickly to clear the tears that threatened to spill from his eyes.

Emily watched her boys and knew exactly how they felt.

George grasped the arms of the chair and pulled himself upward when he saw a woman walking in their direction. Across from him, the outdated woman's magazine in Rose's hands slipped to the floor as she too, rose. Tyler and Tanner swiveled in place, instinctively moved closer to each other, crossed their arms over their chest and cocked their head in the same direction. Dave and Emily were the last to stand. Dave put his hand under Emily's arm, brushed his lips across her hair, pulled her upward to meet the newcomer.

"I'm Marcy, I'm a surgical nurse here. Are you the O'Brien family?"

"How's my daughter? Is she going to be okay? Was she wearing a helmet?" Dave fired a succession of questions, impatient for answers. Emily waited by his side, her hand tightly wrapped around his upper arm, drawing shaky breaths, as they waited for her reply.

"A helmet?" Marcy eyebrows went up and then she took a deep breath. "I don't think you folks have been told exactly what happened to your daughter. I apologize…"

"I just assumed she was hit by a car. She rides a bike and she was going to the bookstore earlier this morning. It was dark. I shouldn't have let her go. George called and said she was injured. I just assumed…" Dave's voice drifted off.

Marcy stared from one family member to the next. The second hand on the oversized clock behind them made a soft clunk, and then another, before she opened her mouth to speak. "Your daughter was shot."

Emily took a staggering step backwards. "What do you mean shot?"

George glanced at Rose before looking down and shaking his head slowly.

Dave threw his arm and stabilized his wife who leaned into him heavily. "She's going to be alright, Emmie."

"But she hasn't said that, she hasn't told us how she is doing." Emily's expression crumpled and she turned to press her face into Dave's upper arm. Dave looked over his wife's hair and met Marcy's eyes.

"Is she alright?" he croaked.

Marcy returned the questioning gaze, feeling guilty that she could not provide any comfort to the family. "I don't know... I'm sorry. She still in surgery, as soon as we get any information, I'll come and talk to you." Marcy reached out, squeezed Emily's hand and Emily smiled weakly at the reassurance.

"This must be the family I've been looking for..."

Marcy turned with a smile at the older gentleman holding a crumbled face mask in his hand. "I'm Dr. Mack and I'm sure you've been waiting to hear from me." Marcy tried to step away from the family but found her hand was still taken up in Emily's firm grasp. She angled to Emily's left to allow the surgeon to stand in front of the family.

Seeing the tangled arms, Dr Mack lightly touched Emily's arm and replaced Marcy's hand with his own. "Let's have a seat and I'll give you an update on your daughter." He guided the family to their seats again.

## CHAPTER FORTY-THREE

"I guess she was in the wrong spot at the wrong time, Rose."

Rose choked a little as she responded to Dave, "She's lucky to be alive."

"I know, believe me, I know."

Maddy yawned as she woke, stretched her arms over her head and felt a pulling at her right side. With hands that felt weak and shaky, she lifted the stiff sheet and peered down at the thick white bandages that criss-crossed over her abdomen. Alarmed now, she tried to sit up and the twinge at her side exploded into fiery heat that brought bile to her throat. Her breath caught, she collapsed backward and closed her eyes against the pain.

"Are you hurting? Should I get the nurse?" Rose was the first to notice Maddy's distress as she woke up. She pushed the nurse's call button on the side of the bed *several* times and then walked to the doorway to peer down both sides of the long hallway. Seeing no one, Rose took another worried glance at Maddy before leaving in pursuit of help. Her dad reached over the bedrail, used the edge of the sheet to dab at the tears flowing down her cheeks.

"He came after me." Maddy's throat was dry, painful and her voice cracked as she spoke.

"What?" Her dad leaned in, his expression troubled.

"He was there on purpose. Mr. Sheldon came after me."

"What are you saying, Maddy?" His hand paused in the act of adjusting her sheets.

"He was going after Sloane...and me."

"What? Why, Maddy?'

"Because of what Sloane knew about the missing girls... and because of what I saw." Maddy voice dropped to a whisper and she closed her eyes for a moment.

"What you saw, Maddy?" His hand tightened on the sheet.

"I saw the girl die, dad. I saw the man shoot her in the street."

Maddy's dad ran his hands through his already mussed hair. His fingers shook as he replaced them on the bed rail. He was quiet for a moment, finally asked the question.

"Why didn't you tell me?"

A minute passed when they both listened to the monotonous drone of the heating unit and the soft patter of footsteps outside in the hallway.

"Would you have believed me?"

Maddy's dad was not surprised by the question but she could see the flash of pain in his eyes before he looked away, out the large window that ran the length of the room.

"I don't know, Maddy." His voice was raw, gravelly, and when he finally returned her gaze she saw that his eyes were moist.

Maddy felt a warmth in her chest, took a deep breath of the sterile hospital air and felt different, unconstrained and relaxed. She wondered if being a sentira meant that she was not only more aware of evil but also its opposite, *goodness*.

"It's okay dad, I understand."

"I<small>T WAS A CLOSE GAME</small>, the weather held out till the end."

"Yeah, that last field goal was a game changer."

"Did you get your homework finished?"

"Ah, mom…."

"Be a bit quieter, Tanner, you'll wake her up."

"She sure does sleep a lot."

"She's healing and the pain medicine makes her sleepy."

Maddy lay in bed with her eyes closed and listened to the voices swirling around her. It was an odd thing, feeling invisible and yet able to sense the soul threads that tethered one family member to another. She felt she was caught, *cocooned* really, right in the middle of them all.

"I<small>S</small> she going to be alright? Is there anything Thomas or I can do?" Sarah whispered the words while her eyes cut to the right and took in the rumpled sheets, beeping monitors and sleeping girl. "I can't believe this, she was *shot?*"

"We don't want to intrude on your family, we just wanted to drop off some flowers for Maddy." Thomas stood, with his wife, at the room's entrance with a floral arrangement that was almost as wide as the doorway. He craned his head around the spiky gladiolas rising from the center of the design.

"Thomas, Sarah, nice to see you again. You just missed Emily and Rose, they're on chauffeur duty for the boys. Let me help you with those. Maddy will love them." George rose from the vinyl recliner closest to the door and reached out to take the large arrangement. Once in his hands, he rotated in place, searching for an empty spot in a room whose few flat surfaces were already filled with stuffed animals, get well cards and balloon bouquets.

Sarah slid past Thomas and pointed to a spot on the floor by the door. "Put them down, George. I don't know what we were thinking. The same thing happened when my mom had her last surgery, we had a roomful of plants and gifts. Thomas and I will take this by the house, we can take a few of the other gifts too, so that you don't have as much to manage when she's discharged. Now, back to the important stuff, how is she?"

"She's going to be fine. The surgeon is happy with her progress, she's been up walking a little, they removed her drain today ...and some of those blasted monitors that beep all night." Dave smiled as he looked over to the bed where Maddy lay undisturbed by the conversation around her.

"So, will she get to go home soon?" Sarah wandered closer to the girl, noting how pale and fragile she looked against the starched white hospital sheets. Her fingers trailed down Maddy's arm, shuddering when she encountered the IV site and her mind made uncomfortable comparisons with her own daughter. Ashton's hair had the same length and curl, blonde instead of auburn. And she had the same innocent look when she slept, the same fringe of long lashes that fanned on her cheeks. *This could be my daughter... this could have happened to us.* Her eyes rose and captured her husband's and she could tell by the stark look on his face that he was thinking the same thing.

"Yeah, we think so. They just want to make sure she doesn't start bleeding again. She lost a lot of blood with the nick to her liver but they expect it'll heal nicely and she'll make a full recovery." Dave motioned toward the two chairs in the room but Thomas and Sarah both shook their heads and made their way back to the door. Thomas lifted his hand to wave goodbye, reminded Dave to call if he needed anything, leaned over, picked up the arrangement and followed Sarah out the door.

## CHAPTER FORTY-FOUR

*M*orghan's hand trembled when she reached for the gray silk blouse and pulled it off the hanger. Black was out of the question. She would not mourn Blane, *not after what he did*, but a somber approach was definitely called for. Gray was appropriate, respectable and most importantly, already in her closet, because she had no time for shopping or any other preparation. Everything was in disarray. Everything hinged on what happened today. Her place in the community, the donations to the teen center, the *future* of the teen center itself rested on what happened next.

She nodded thoughtfully at her image in the mirror, the modest silver jewelry worked well with the gray outfit, her makeup was light enough for the dark circles to be visible, and the strands of hair that drifted out of her classic style gave her a fragile, guileless look. Wishing she had more time to prepare, she called out to her daughter and headed toward the car.

It was immediately clear that no one recognized her when Morghan entered the hospital room. Dave and Emily were sitting in the vinyl recliners that flanked the window and Morghan saw them make eye contact with each other before looking over to Maddy. Maddy's expression remained puzzled until Allison stepped from behind her mother and hurried toward the hospital bed. Dave's gaze bounced back and forth between the occupants of the room while Emily's eyes remained steadfastly on Morghan.

"I hope I'm not interrupting?" Morghan asked in a quiet voice.

"No…nothing's going on at the moment. I'm afraid I don't know you?" Dave stood, confused at the fleeting expressions on his daughter's face. Recognition, confusion and maybe even fear. "Are you one of Maddy's friends?" he asked Allison.

Allison opened her mouth to answer but Morghan stepped forward, in front of her, and started her explanation. "I'm Morghan Sheldon and this is my daughter, Allison." Dave flinched and his eyes widened in recognition of the name but she took a deep breath and went on grimly. "I'm here to say how very, very sorry I am for my husband's actions. I want you to know that I am horrified by what has happened and I would not blame you if you asked us to leave. But we had to come here and make sure that Maddy's going to be okay." Morghan's lashes sparkled with unshed tears and a red flush blossomed on her cheeks. She returned Dave's guarded stare briefly but shifted to bear the brunt of Emily's scrutiny. With unwavering eyes and hands that trembled she held out a small package with a lavish bow. "It's chocolate, Allison says she likes….."

"Uhh, I'm not sure…" Dave stammered as glanced from Emily back to Morghan.

Emily launched out of the chair, strode across the room, and positioned herself in front of the newcomer with her hands on her hips. She leaned forward with narrowed eyes.

"Are you telling me that you did not know what was going on at that teen shelter?"

"What *is* going on is that girls are getting off the street and getting the help they need. Beyond that, I'm in the dark as much as you are. Blane was up to something and he did some horrible, unforgivable things, including hurting your daughter, but Allison and I are victims too. We had no idea what was going on." Morghan spoke with measured words in a voice that was both soft and unyielding.

Maddy shoved herself up in bed. She had not seen her mother that angry since, well, maybe never. Her eyes widened as she watched the exchange, ignoring Allison who stood by her side, equally engrossed in the conversation. She could tell by the expression on her dad's face, and his more relaxed stance, that he believed Allison's mom. Her mom took longer to convince but Maddy knew the worst was over when her mom took several tissues out of her purse and pushed them into Morghan's hand. A wary, tingly feeling climbed up Maddy's spine and she felt a queasiness in her stomach while she watched the adults talking, but a tugging on her arm distracted her from following the adult's conversation any further.

"My mother is going to take me shopping." Allison leaned down to whisper conspiratorially into Maddy's ear. "She going to buy me real clothes so I don't look like I go to private school anymore. Jeans, boots...." Allison's eyes glowed with excitement and she leaned over the give Maddy a spontaneous hug. She didn't see Maddy wince when her elbow pushed into the bandaged side, nor did she seem to notice Maddy's strained smile. "We can be friends again, Maddy."

# CHAPTER FORTY-FIVE

*M*addy realized she had fallen asleep again when she heard the soft murmuring of voices in the room. She stretched, stopped in apprehension when she remembered her side, but continued to slowly spread her arms overhead, pleased that she was moving with less pain.

"I've been thinking that we should take a drive and visit another fire station"

"I would like to see Station 8, George. It was built in 1925 and the last fire station to stable horses."

"Hey, isn't that the one on Trenton? I don't think it's a fire station anymore TJ, they revitalized it into an advertising agency."

*So cold.* The shivering started with her toes. When she pulled the blanket closer to her neck, her feet peeked out below and chills marched up her body until her teeth chattered. George swiveled in the chair when he heard the miserable noise she was making. He put down the book he was reading and walked over toward her. She squinted at the bright light streaming through the window behind him and then closed her eyes, more in frustration than pain.

"Let me see if I can get another blanket, Madison, sweet-ie." George paused at the door, craned his head in both direc-tions, and lumbered down the corridor.

TJ put one sneaker, then the other, on the bottom rung of the metal side rails of Maddy's bed. Balancing precariously, he gripped the rail with his one hand, leaned over and shook her shoulder impatiently with the other. The rail clattered against the frame, and the nurse call button fell to the floor with a thunk. "Maddy, open your eyes! We need to talk."

Maddy opened her eyes and sighed when she saw the young boy's face mere inches from her own. He took his hand off her shoulder, used it to swipe the hair out of his eyes, looked at her with an earnest, serious expression and then fell backward onto the linoleum floor. Maddy muttered under her breath, curled her hand around the bedrail and slowly pulled herself up. Her abdominal muscles spasmed so it took a moment and a deep breath before she could speak. "Are you okay, TJ?"

TJ nodded. He blinked the strands of hair out of his eyes and jumped to his feet. Cupping his hand to his mouth, he leaned forward over the bedrail and whispered.

"I saw unicorns, Maddy."

# CHAPTER FORTY-SIX

*T*ulsa **World-November 29 edition**
A full investigation of the teen shelter murders was concluded today and a frustratingly small amount of information was ultimately discovered. A local girl, who because of her age, will remain unnamed, discovered that Blane Sheldon was responsible for homeless girls being kidnapped from his own teen shelter.

Earlier, Sheldon had suggested that his employee was trying to save one of the girls when both the teen and the man were found murdered in front of the shelter last month. The local girl's story contradicts Sheldon's, and she remains the sole witness to the assault. She testified that the employee actually shot and killed the teenager when the young lady attempted escape. A fight ensued between two male employees and one man struck and killed the other with a car.

She further claims that Blane Sheldon discovered she had information on the kidnappings, that he and another unknown assailant followed her to the alley behind the bookshop on Cherry Street. It was there that they confronted and attacked her.

The young girl lost consciousness when she was struck by a bullet and suffered a life-threatening injury. She is unable to provide any details about the incident but is expected to make a full recovery. Presumably, another fight broke out in the alley and Blane Sheldon was killed.

Morghan Sheldon was recently seen leaving the police station, her elegant face a mixture of loss and bewilderment. There has been no information to date that demonstrates she had any part of the abhorrent situation. On the contrary, she appears to be yet another victim of her husband's greed and deceit. During an interview with Mrs. Sheldon, she expressed profound sympathy for all those that have been hurt by her husband and she prays for healing and peace to be restored to the community she has come to love.

"MORGHAN, this is Thomas Markham, you might remember me from the Alliance."

"Thomas, I cannot express how sorry I am. I feel so humiliated by my husband's actions."

"Morghan, no one holds you responsible. The investigation demonstrated that you had no idea what Blane was doing. I am reaching out to you today to see what your plans are. Specifically, what you plan to do about the teen shelter. I know that you're probably feeling over your head right now so I'm calling to offer our support. It would be a shame to close the center when you've made so much progress."

"You have no idea how your words comfort me. I've been losing so much sleep over this. I don't want the teens or the shelter to suffer for the actions of my husband. What do you suggest Thomas?"

"Why don't you look at when you could meet with the committee and outline what your needs are. We can see what type of support we can offer until the situation stabilizes. Judging from the calls I am receiving, you have quite a few supporters who want to make sure that you, and the shelter, weather this storm."

"I'll do that Thomas. It will be so good for me to focus on something positive instead of the deception that was my marriage. Thank you for your phone call."

# CHAPTER FORTY-SEVEN

*M*addy woke, disoriented, in the dark room. As her eyes adjusted, she recognized the books stacked haphazardly on her bedside table, the curves of the antique iron bedrails and the soft whine of one of the dogs on the floor underneath her. She snuggled deeper into the flannel sheets and closed her eyes again but Zeus only whined louder and then stuck his wet nose in her ear. She twisted her head and he caught her eye, thumped his tail loudly on the floor, continued his incessant whine.

Maddy looked up at the ceiling, thought about calling for her parents but then remembered how tired they looked when they all finally came home from the hospital earlier that day. She yanked back the blankets instead, held her right hand over her bandages and slowly lowered her feet to the floor. She donned her sweat shirt and slipped on a pair of furry slippers she'd abandoned at the foot of the bed. Movements still caused a tugging, pinching sensation so she took slow shuffling steps to the stairwell. Zeus ran past her, turned to look up at her, his tongue lolling and tail thumping against the side wall. She gripped the handrail and took the first step down.

She had no time to celebrate her small accomplishment of descending the stairs before Zeus was directing her toward the door. A breeze, smelling of wood smoke, rushed over her face, roused her from her drowsiness when she opened the door. Zeus barked loudly, and she stepped outside, worried he would wake the neighbors.

He made no move to run to the grass but sat patiently waiting for her approach. With each step, his body quivered until finally he bounded forward in an exuberant lunge and pranced around her feet. Maddy was puzzled. She tried to touch the top of his head but he leapt away and bolted toward the driveway, looking backward at her with mirthful eyes. The twisting motion brought a sharp pain to her side and she lowered her head and muttered creative curses at the runaway dog.

Maddy's eyes widened when warm air feathered over the top of her head. She swiped at her damp lashes with the back of her hand and looked up. He was magnificent, as always. She took a tentative step and placed her cheek against his warm neck.

"Good evening, milady. I am much relieved that you are looking better."

"Thank you Silenus." Maddy reached out and gingerly ran her hand along an angry slash on his flank. "Does it hurt?"

"Yes, but like your injury, it will heal with time."

"Another mark of valor for both of us, huh?" Maddy's mouth curved up in a wry smile as her hand moved up and down stroking his long neck.

"Yes, Madison." He paused, turned his head and met her eye. "I am quite proud of you. I have to say, I never doubted your courage."

"You may not have, but I sure did." Maddy paused, looked

up into the sky where stars peeked between the broken clouds. "How'd you know I could do it?"

"You are a sentira, your whole essence reacts against evil and by your very nature, you are protective of those around you. There was no other path for you, you knew that the girls' fate was in your hands. You are simply incapable of ignoring the needs of others.

Maddy returned his gaze and nodded slowly. "What happens next?"

"I will continue training to ready myself to protect and defend." He narrowed his eyes and stared at her for a moment. "And you, sentira, I have a feeling that destiny still has plans for you. You are quite a special girl, Madison, and you will make an extraordinary woman."

"You're leaving me...forever?" Maddy leaned her forehead into Silenus' side. She reached upward to tightly grab a fistful of mane and ignored the stretching ache in her side.

"We will always be connected, Madison, by ties that cannot be broken. If you encounter danger, I will be at your side." Silenus took a step back and met her eyes one more time. He nodded to her and she returned his gaze with shimmering eyes before finally nodding back.

Silenus' mane swirled as he swung his head and turned his body toward the street. The unicorns she had seen earlier, the smaller dappled grey and the mahogany with the bronze horn, appeared from nowhere and took up their places on either side of Silenus. Street lights picked up the sheen of their horns as they passed underneath but their hooves made no noise as they quickened their gait to a trot.

Maddy watched the trio as they advanced in the darkness and became shadows themselves. She shivered, wrapped her arms around herself and then turned to walk up the driveway toward the house. Zeus appeared at her side again. He swished his tail a couple times then bumped her legs gently as they walked together toward the kitchen. Maddy winced as she pulled on the door but then smiled again as she entered the warm room.

Silenus' mane rippled down his back, he shook his head and burst into a gallop down the dark street. The mahogany and smaller unicorn followed suit and easily matched his tempo, their stride increasing until their gallop equalled the speed of the very wind around them. Leaves gave up their tenuous grip on branches above and drifted and swirled on the ground beneath their hooves. The unicorns cut through the thickening fog and as they rode, their forms transformed from solid to become part of the mist itself. The vapor had all but swallowed them when the smaller unicorn pulled up abruptly, raised up on his hind legs, flattened his ears and neighed loudly, wildly. He circled urgently, created more eddies in the fog as he peered into the darkness. Light from lamps above fought the mist and flashed on his silver horn. Coming full circle and seeing nothing, he surged ahead in the direction that Silenus and the mahogany had taken and then he too, disappeared in the haze.

# AFTERWORD

**Could you help me out?**

This book is self-published and depends on word-of-mouth to find new readers. **Could you take a moment and give this book a review?**

Ebook readers, click HERE!

**Did I do it?**

Did I make you wish, just for a moment, that unicorns were real? You should try writing about them! In the beginning I just wanted an original name for an imaginary creature, but by the end, Silenus was making corrections to his own dialogue.

*From the dusty pages of myths and fables, unicorns are coming back to life. You can be there and watch it happen.*

ALSO BY SUSAN BADARACCO

**The Oath Series**

The Oath: Ashton and Egorn

(An introduction to the next book follows this page…)

The Oath: Maribella and Connery

The Oath: The Death of Magic

**The Nine Jewels Series**

The Nine Jewels

Akbar's Diamond

The reading list for each series can be found on:
Susanbadaracco.com

**Susan Badaracco** is the author and independent publisher of The Oath series and The Nine Jewels series.

She likes hot tea, finding a perfect shade of lipstick, learning to make pretzels and enjoying lunch dates with girlfriends.

She lives with her husband and a cat named Tass— short for Catastrophe. The cat is naughty, but they put up with her anyway. Her husband refuses to discuss any future pets.

# The Oath
## Ashton and Egorn

# SUSAN
# BADARACCO

## ASHTON AND EGORN

*E*gorn's decision to go to battle saved his life.

Only a sliver of a moon lit the otherwise dark night when he heard the rustling of the others making preparations. He kept his eyes closed, feigning sleep, until the neighing and the shuffling noises died down. Once he deemed it safe, he crept around the sleeping families, following the same path as the warriors. He dare not let anyone see him. He had to get to the battlefield where he would prove his worth and avenge his father's death. It was his sacred duty. Once he did that, they would be forced to acknowledge his superior skills as a soldier, allow him the right to engage in combat like the others. He'd dutifully paid attention to all of the lectures, participated in all of their drills and while he wasn't as massive as Silenus or Garrick… he was ready.

His heart leapt with emotion and pride when the warrior unicorns thundered down the first knoll. The earth quaked underfoot, sending exhilarating vibrations through his body and reminding him that this was real—he was headed for battle.

It wasn't long, however, before he fell behind. Far behind. His stamina, he admitted to himself, was not equal to the more experienced soldiers. He'd need to work on that. Or risk getting lost. Like he was now.

Egorn was so distracted by these thoughts that it took him a moment to recognize the noises. Screeching, ear-splitting neighing and the cracking of horns. He followed the commotion with his heart rising up in his throat and a steely resolve in his eye.

Shouldering his way through the shrubbery and low hanging branches he emerged to a chilling sight. The enemy —coming directly at him. At least a dozen. He froze, wide-eyed, his heart pounding in his chest.

"Horn! Horn!"

Egorn heard the command in the uproar and remembered his drills. When confronting the enemy, you must position your head correctly to attack with your horn. He gulped, lowered his head, and then...closed his eyes in terror.

GARRICK WAS ENGAGED in battle when he saw his opponent suddenly stand down, turn and then run laterally toward a grove of trees. A quick glance confirmed that the rest of the unit was having the same experience. The enemy was disengaging. He was the leader of these unicorns, an accomplished warrior and he'd never seen this happen before. He hesitated, reflecting on the withdrawal. *What is the meaning of this?* His pondering was interrupted by an alarming sight— Egorn, a young unicorn from the village, emerging from the trees.

"Egorn! Egorn!" he yelled, alerting the rest of the unit. All eyes turned in the same direction and immediately the warriors bolted into action to save the youngster. There was absolutely no chance for any of them to reach Egorn in time, the distance was too great. Garrick forced himself to watch.

The youngster visibly shuddered before lowering his head. The sun's rays twinkled on the burnished silver of his horn, splashed light on the trees limbs above. Garrick slammed the ground with his foreleg and steeled himself against the bloody reality about to unfold. For a long moment, the dust from the stampeding warriors obstructed his view. By the time it settled, the enemy had scattered in the copse and Egorn was left untouched.

Garrick let out his breath with a groan, flattened his ears and swished his tail violently. It made no sense. Why was Egorn alive? Unicorn warriors rushed to gather around the youth, reassuring themselves that he had come to no harm. They shuffled backward, opening the ring, as Garrick approached with his heavy hoofbeats and stern expression.

"What is this about? Who gave you permission to accompany us into battle?"

No one had, of course. Egorn lowered his head in shame. Criticism rained down on him from the warriors surrounding him protectively. His eyes welled up with tears but he clenched them tight and tried to hide his distress.

"That's enough." Silenus' low voice was enough to quiet the clamor. "I imagine if anything is going to teach young Egorn a lesson, this near miss was probably sufficient." He turned to Garrick, "Shall we return? There does not appear to be anything left to do here."

Garrick issued the command, the troops fell in line and they started the trot towards home.

∾

EGORN FOLLOWED THE WARRIORS, breathing in the dust stirred up by their massive hooves. By the time they approached the village, he had a fine coat of dirt covering his pewter grey hide and an itch in his nose. He was going to be in big trouble. He slowed his pace to contemplate the situation. There was the possibility that his mother would be relieved to see him, perhaps she thought him missing and was worried, perhaps she would cry out in joy...

Egorn noticed that the warriors had stopped on the crest overlooking the meadow. This was it, then. He had often climbed the opposite side to meet the returning unicorns with the rest of the families. His mother was likely approaching or even talking to Garrick now. He pranced in agitation and then rushed up the final ascent to face whatever would come.

As Egorn neared the top, Garrick turned abruptly and motioned to Connery, an older warrior. "Stay with him," he commanded. The remaining unicorns charged down the hill, snorting and squealing. Egorn stood stock still. It was as if the warriors were attacking their own families. Connery eyed Egorn sympathetically but barred him from reaching the top so he could see what was going on. "Stay back lad, we've had our orders," he said gruffly. Egorn's day had already been quite long and frustrating. He put down his head in submission to the older unicorn—then in a blink, bolted to the side and over the crest.

Egorn knew that he would never forget the sight for the rest of his life. Unicorns, previously dove white, were laying in scattered positions in the field in front of him, bloodied and still. The warriors were galloping, prancing, and snorting in distress. At their feet lay their wives, sisters and children.

Egorn felt Connery's presence by his side and together the two unicorns slowly descended the hill. His head felt strange, airy, as he walked among the dead with their shredded hides and blank stares. They plodded slowly, stepping over twisted limbs and puddles of thick red liquid.

In time, Connery shouldered Egorn and announced gravely, "We're here."

Egorn spun around and looked at the older unicorn in confusion. "Where? What are you talking about?"

Connery tilted his head toward the mangled bodies in front of them.

Egorn shook his head wildly, lifted up on his hind legs, neighed in protest.

"Look at her leg." Egorn's mother had a scar running down the length of her left foreleg, an injury from her childhood. It was undeniable. The body next to hers, his baby sister. The air rushed out of Egorn's thickened throat with a harsh whinny. He stumbled on his feet and almost pitched to the ground. Garrick arrived at that moment and pressed his massive body against Egorn's side while Connery stabilized the opposite side.

"Easy, lad, we've got you."

"My mother…my sister…"

"They died quickly with no pain," Garrick was quick to declare.

Human women carrying baskets of liniments and bandages streamed into the field ready to clean and bandage wounded unicorns as they did after all battles. Their actions were symbolic. The unicorn's own life force, the victus sitis, would restore the warriors to full health in very little time. But the townspeople wanted to reciprocate for the good deeds the unicorns offered freely on a regular basis. Unicorn tears could heal any injury or illness and they were generous with their magic.

Upon their stunned recognition of the dead, their useless supplies were dropped and forgotten in the grassy meadow.

Instead, funeral pyres were organized, graves being an impossibility with the sheer numbers of the slain. While younger warriors galloped across the fields flashing horns in the afternoon sun, older unicorns bent their heads low in sorrow. The deaths of the innocents forced both unicorn and human to reflect upon the same question. What would happen to the unicorn race?

As the day melted into evening, the townspeople tended funeral fires that dotted the valley and whose flames licked the skies. The warriors gathered to the side of the humans, regarding the pyres as they discussed the atrocity. Their voices, harsh and rowdy, floated in the evening breezes carrying words like justice, honor and retribution. Connery and Silenus stood side by side, silently watching the agitation escalate.

"It will never end, you know," said Connery.

"It ends for me tonight," replied Silenus, his voice hard.

Garrick tried, unsuccessfully, to urge the younger warriors to curb their bloodlust. "You must separate your pain and lock it away." Egorn thrashed his head and stomped his hooves roughly into the soil still moist with the blood of the slain. He ignored his leader's pleas, demanded the right to accompany the unit who claimed they would seek vengeance for those who murdered innocents and annihilated all of their futures.

As the stars dusted the skies, the men from the village herded their families together for the return trip home. Younger children were picked up and squeezed a little tighter while older ones looked over their shoulders in apprehension despite all adult reassurances.

Egorn watched Silenus deftly maneuver past high-strung unicorns and retreating humans before coming to a stop before a young girl. Her blonde hair glowed and the tears on her cheeks shimmered with the reflected light of the funeral pyres. Egorn recognized Clara even from the distance of the meadow. Best friend to Silenus' daughter, she used to braid daisies and buttercups into Flora's snowy mane.

*What is he doing?* Egorn thought, and then gasped. After a brief discussion with Clara's father, Silenus was bowing down to the young girl. This was unheard of, fundamentally wrong. Silenus was a leader of warriors and this child was... nothing. He watched Clara touch Silenus' horn and stretch her arms around his neck. Before Egorn could make any sense of what just happened, Connery bowed down before *another* girl. By this time, both humans and unicorns gathered in hushed fascination to see the massive warriors pay homage the young girls.

Egorn was struck by the significance of the event but was drawn away again with the clamor of angry voices. Aldrich's gravelly voice rose above the others and Egorn listened intently, nodding his head in agreement and stomping his hoof in affirmation. It was his destiny to avenge his *whole* family now, to search out and destroy the marauders and Aldrich had a plan to do just that.

It was only when the fires disintegrated to blood red embers and the harsh snorting and thrashing died down, that Egorn finally gave in to the soul wrenching weariness of the day. He laid down to rest, not by his mother's warm side— that would never happen again—but amongst warriors bent on retribution.

But when the sun crested the horizon the next morning, he found himself alone.

Aldrich's squad had departed some time earlier, leaving the younger unicorn behind. He bolted to his feet, circled the meadow and frantically galloped toward the hill. His lungs strained and legs burned with the speed of his ascent. Once he reached the rise, he swiveled in place but there was nothing to indicate the direction of the missing warriors.

Egorn's ears flattened back and his eyes went wide and wild. Lifting up on his hind legs, he screamed out his frustration, thrashed his horn side to side. Next, he galloped across the ridge in short bursts, snorting and spewing, until his legs threatened to buckle. Below him, Silenus and Connery's head swiveled as they silently regarded his show of temper. Still puffing furiously, Egorn dropped his head and made the slow descent down the rise until he stood before the warriors.

"I will destroy them. It's my right!"

Silenus waited a long moment. Egorn finally lifted his head and glared.

Silenus' voice was quiet, reasonable. "It is your right, Egorn. But you're not ready. Would it not be better to give yourself time to become the warrior you are destined to be?"

"But I'm ready *now*."

Connery's bronze horn flashed before striking Egorn's smaller silver horn. The young unicorn's head whipped to the side with the blow, he stumbled and would've tumbled to the ground were it not for Silenus who stepped forward to brace him.

"No, you are not," Connery replied drily. Turning, he stepped away from the unicorn whose eyes returned down to his hooves. "But you will be."

THERE WERE two reactions to the massacre.

Most of the unicorns joined Aldrich and plotted revenge. They banded together and scoured the countryside. When they found the enemy warriors that had destroyed their homes and families, they were ruthless.

The remaining unicorns recognized that revenge was not a strong enough force to counteract their indescribable grief. They swore to fiercely protect that which they had failed to safeguard that reprehensible day—the blameless, the virtuous. And so an Oath was made that day from warriors to innocents, a pledge that continues till this day.

THE OATH: Ashton and Egorn can be found on Amazon.